The T[...]sh

And Other [...]dia
Collected [...] ROOKE
And Retold by
W·H·D·ROUSE
Illustrated by W.H. Robinson.

The Talking Thrush
And Other Tales from India

"A Crow is a Crow for ever."

Preface

THE stories contained in this little book are only a small part of a large collection of Indian folk-tales, made by Mr. Crooke in the course of the Ethnological Survey of the North-West Provinces and Oudh. Some were recorded by the collector from the lips of the jungle-folk of Mirzápur; others by his native assistant, Pandit Rámgharíb Chaubé. Besides these, a large number were received from all parts of the Provinces in response to a circular issued by Mr. J. C. Nesfield, the Director of Public Instruction, to all teachers of village schools.

The present selection is confined to the Beast Stories, which are particularly interesting as being mostly indigenous and little affected by so-called Aryan influence. Most of them are new, or have been published only in the *North Indian Notes and Queries* (referred to as *N.I.N.Q.*).

In the re-telling, for which Mr. Rouse is responsible, a number of changes have been made. The text of the book is meant for children, and consequently the first aim has been to make an interesting story. Those who study folk-tales for any scientific purpose will find all such changes marked in the Notes. If the change is considerable, the original document is summarised. It should be added that these documents are merely brief Notes in themselves, without literary interest. The Notes also give the source of each tale, and a few obvious parallels, or references to the literature of the subject.

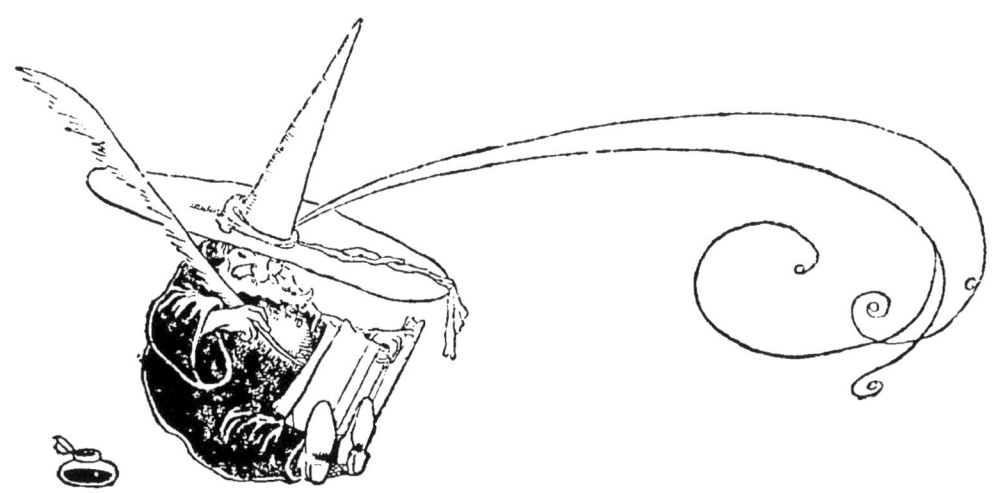

Contents

	PAGE
THE TALKING THRUSH	1
THE RABBIT AND THE MONKEY	8
THE SPARROW'S REVENGE	16
THE JUDGMENT OF THE JACKAL	21
HOW THE MOUSE GOT INTO HIS HOLE	25
KING SOLOMON AND THE OWL	30
THE CAMEL'S NECK	33
THE QUAIL AND THE FOWLER	36
THE KING OF THE KITES	39
THE JACKAL AND THE CAMEL	43
THE WISE OLD SHEPHERD	47
BEWARE OF BAD COMPANY	53
THE FOOLISH WOLF	55

Contents

	PAGE
REFLECTED GLORY	58
THE CAT AND THE SPARROWS	61
THE FOOLISH FISH	65
THE CLEVER GOAT	72
A CROW IS A CROW FOR EVER	76
THE GRATEFUL GOAT	81
THE CUNNING JACKAL; OR, THE BITER BIT	85
THE FARMER'S ASS	89
THE PARROT JUDGE	93
THE FROG AND THE SNAKE	97
LITTLE MISS MOUSE AND HER FRIENDS	101
THE JACKAL THAT LOST HIS TAIL	105
THE WILY TORTOISE	110
THE KING OF THE MICE	112
THE VALIANT BLACKBIRD	117
THE GOAT AND THE HOG	123
THE PARROT AND THE PARSON	127
THE LION AND THE HARE	130
THE MONKEY'S BARGAINS	132
THE MONKEY'S REBUKE	139
THE BULL AND THE BULLFINCH	145
THE SWAN AND THE CROW	150
PRIDE SHALL HAVE A FALL	156
THE KID AND THE TIGER	160
THE STAG, THE CROW, AND THE JACKAL	166

Contents

	PAGE
THE MONKEY AND THE CROWS	170
THE SWAN AND THE PADDY-BIRD	173
WHAT IS A MAN?	176
THE WOUND AND THE SCAR	182
THE CAT AND THE PARROT	186
NOTES	195

List of Illustrations

"A Crow is a Crow for Ever"	*Frontispiece*

	PAGE
TITLE-PAGE	v
PREFACE: Headpiece	vii
CONTENTS: Headpiece	ix
,, Tailpiece	xi
THE TALKING THRUSH:	
Initial	1
THE RABBIT AND THE MONKEY:	
Initial	8
Man with Bamboo Pole	9
"Sit in front of that Man"	11
Tailpiece	15
THE SPARROW'S REVENGE:	
"Up jumped the Boy, and out he ran"	19
THE JUDGMENT OF THE JACKAL:	
Initial	21
"The Merchant was much dismayed"	22
"And away they went"	23
HOW THE MOUSE GOT INTO HIS HOLE:	
Initial	25
KING SOLOMON AND THE OWL:	
Initial	30
Tailpiece	32
THE CAMEL'S NECK:	
Headpiece	33
THE QUAIL AND THE FOWLER:	
Headpiece	36
Tailpiece	38

List of Illustrations

	PAGE
THE BULL AND THE BULLFINCH:	
Initial	145
Tailpiece	149
THE SWAN AND THE CROW:	
Initial	150
"Hm, hm," said the Judge, looking at the Crow	153
Tailpiece	155
PRIDE SHALL HAVE A FALL:	
Initial	156
Tailpiece	159
THE KID AND THE TIGER:	
Initial	160
THE STAG, THE CROW, AND THE JACKAL:	
Initial	166
Tailpiece	169
THE MONKEY AND THE CROWS:	
"O Monkey, what a fool you must be!"	171
Tailpiece	172
THE SWAN AND THE PADDY-BIRD:	
Initial	173
Tailpiece	175
WHAT IS A MAN:	
"He espied an Elephant"	178
"I am a Man," said the other	180
THE WOUND AND THE SCAR:	
Initial	182
Tailpiece	185
THE CAT AND THE PARROT:	
"The Cat said to the Parrot, Come, friend"	187
"An old woman happened to be near"	191
FINIS	218

The Talking Thrush

A CERTAIN man had a garden, and in his garden he sowed cotton seeds. By-and-by the cotton seeds grew up into a cotton bush, with big brown pods upon it. These pods burst open when they are ripe; and you can see the fluffy white cotton bulging all white out of the pods. There was a Thrush in this garden, and the Thrush thought within herself how nice and soft the cotton looked. She plucked out some of it to line her nest with; and never before was her sleep so soft as it was on that bed of cotton.

Now this Thrush had a clever head; so she thought something more might be done with cotton besides lining a nest. In her flights abroad she used often to pass by the door of a Cotton-carder. The Cotton-carder had a thing like a bow, made of a piece of wood, and a thong of leather tying the ends together into a curve. He used to take the cotton, and pile it in a heap; then he took the carding-bow, and twang-twang-twanged it among the heap of cotton, so that the fibres or threads of it became disentangled. Then he rolled it up into oblong balls, and sold it to other people, who made it into thread.

The Thrush often watched the Cotton-carder at work. Every day after dinner, she went to the cotton tree, and plucked out a fluff of cotton in her beak and hid it away. She went on doing this till at last she had quite a little heap of cotton all of her own. At least, it was not really her own, because she stole it; but then you cannot get policemen to take up a Thrush for stealing, and as men catch Thrushes and put them in a cage all for nothing, it is only fair the birds should have their turn.

When the heap of cotton was big enough, our Thrush flew to the house of the Cotton-carder, and sat down in front of him.

"Good day, Man," said the Thrush.

"Good day, Birdie," said the Cotton-carder. The Thrush was not a bit afraid, because she knew he was a kind man, who never caught little birds to put them in a cage. He liked better to hear them singing free in the woods.

"Man," said the Thrush, "I have a heap of beautiful cotton, and I'll tell you what. You shall have half of it, if you will card the rest and make it up into balls for me."

"That I will," said the man; "where is it?"

"If you will come with me," said the Thrush, "I'll show you."

So the Thrush flew in front, and the man followed after, and they came to the place where the hoard of cotton was hidden away. The man took the cotton home, and carded it, and made it into balls. Half of the cotton he took for his trouble, and the rest he gave back to the Thrush. He was so honest that he did not cheat even a bird, although he could easily have done so. For birds cannot count : and if you find a nest full of eggs, and take one or two, the mother-bird will never miss them ; but if you take all, the bird is unhappy.

Not far away from the Carder lived a Spinner. This man used to put a ball of cotton on a stick, and then he pulled out a bit of the cotton without breaking it, and tied it to another little stick with a weight on it. Then he twisted the weight, and set it a-spinning ; and as it span, he held the cotton ball in one hand, and pulled out the cotton with the other, working it between finger and thumb to keep it fine. Thus the spindle went on spinning, and the cotton went on twisting, until it was twisted into thread. That is why the man was called a Spinner. It looks very easy to do, when you can do it; but it is really very hard to do well.

To this Spinner the Thrush came, and after bidding him good day, said she—

"Mr. Spinner, I have some balls of cotton all ready to spin into thread. Will you spin one half of them into thread for me, if I give you the other half?"

"That I will," said Mr. Spinner ; and away they went to find the cotton balls, Thrush first and Spinner following.

In a very few days the Spinner had spun all the cotton into the finest thread. Then he took a pair of scales, and weighed it into two equal parts (he was an honest man, too) : half he kept for himself, and the other half he gave to the Thrush.

The next thing this clever Thrush did was to fly to the house of a Weaver. The Weaver used to buy thread, and fasten a number of threads to a wooden frame, called a loom, which was made of two upright posts, with another bar fastened across the top. The threads were hung to the cross-bar, and a little stone was tied to the bottom of each, to keep it steady. Then the Weaver wound some more thread around a long stick called a shuttle; and the shuttle he pushed in front of one thread and behind the next, until it had gone right across the whole of the threads, in and out. Then he pushed it back in the same way, and after a bit, the upright threads and the cross-threads were woven together and made a piece of cloth.

The Thrush flew down to the Weaver, and they made the same bargain as before. The Weaver wove all the thread into pieces of cloth, and half he kept for himself, but the other half he returned to the Thrush.

So now the Thrush had some beautiful cloth, and I dare say you wonder what she wanted it for. As you have not been inquisitive, I will tell you: she wanted clothes to dress herself. The Thrush had noticed that men and women walking about wore clothes, and being an ambitious Thrush, and eager to rise in the world, she felt it would not be proper to go about without any clothes on. So she now went to a Tailor, and said to him—

"Good Mr. Tailor, I have some pieces of very fine cloth, and I should be much obliged if you would make a part of it into clothes for me. You shall have one half of the cloth for your trouble."

The Tailor was very glad of this job, as times were slack. So he took the cloth, and at once set to work. Half of it he made into a beautiful dress for the Thrush, with a skirt and jacket, and sleeves in the latest fashion; and as there was a little cloth left over, and he was an

The Talking Thrush

honest Tailor, he made her also a pretty little hat to put on her head.

Then the Thrush was indeed delighted, and felt there was little more to desire in the world. She put on her skirt, and her jacket with fashionable sleeves, and the little hat, and looked at her image in a river, and was mightily pleased with herself. Now she became so vain that nothing would do, but she must show herself to the King.

So she flew and flew, and away she flew, until she came to the King's palace. Into the King's palace she flew, and into the great hall where the King sat and the Queen and all the courtiers. There was a peg high up on the wall, and the Thrush perched on this peg, and began to sing.

"Oh, look there!" cried the Queen, who was the first to see this wonderful sight—"see, a Thrush in a jacket and skirt and a pretty hat!"

Everybody looked at the Thrush singing on her peg, and clapped their hands.

"Come here, Birdie," said the King, "and show the Queen your pretty clothes."

The Thrush felt highly flattered, and flew down upon the table, and took off her jacket to show the Queen. Then she flew back to her peg, and watched to see what would happen.

The Queen turned over the jacket in her hand, and laughed. Then she folded it up, and put it in her pocket.

"Give me my jacket!" twittered the Thrush. "I shall catch cold, and besides, it is not proper for a lady to be seen without a jacket."

Then they all laughed, and the King said, "Come here, Mistress Thrush, and you shall have your jacket."

Down flew the Thrush upon the table again; but the King caught her, and held her fast.

"Let me go!" squeaked the Thrush, struggling to get free.

But the King would not let her go. I am afraid that although he was a King, he was not so honest as the Carder or the Spinner, and cared less for his word than the Weaver and the Tailor.

"Greedy King," said the Thrush, "to covet my little jacket!"

"I covet more than your jacket," said the King; "I covet you, and I am going to chop you up into little bits."

Then he began to chop her up into bits. As she was being chopped up, the Thrush said, "The King snips and cuts like a Tailor, but he is not so honest!"

When the King had finished chopping her up, he began to wash the pieces. And each piece, as he washed it, called out, "The King scours and scrubs like a washerwoman, but he is not so honest!"

Then the King put the pieces of the Thrush into a frying-pan with oil, and began to fry them. But the pieces went on calling out, "The King is like a cook, frying and sputtering, but he is not so honest!"

When she was fried, the King ate her up. From within the body of the King still the Thrush kept calling out, "I am inside the King! It is just like the inside of any other man, only not so honest!"

The King became like a walking musical-box, and he did not like it at all, but it was his own fault. Wherever

The Talking Thrush

he went, everybody heard the Thrush crying out from inside the King, "Just like any other man, only not so honest!" Everybody that heard this began to despise the King.

At last the King could stand it no longer. He sent for his doctor, and said, "Doctor, you must cut this talking bird out of me."

"Your majesty will die, if I do," said the Doctor.

"I shall die if you don't," answered the King, "for I cannot endure being made a fool of."

So there was nothing for it: the Doctor took his knives, and made a hole in the King, and pulled out the Thrush. Strange to say, the pieces of the Thrush had all joined together again, and away she flew; but her beautiful clothes were all gone. However, it was a lesson she never forgot; and after that, she slept soft in her nest of cotton, and never again tried to ape her betters. As for the King, he died; and a good riddance too.

His son became king in his stead; and all
life long he remembered his father's
miserable death, and kept all his
promises to men, and beasts,
and birds.

The Rabbit and the Monkey

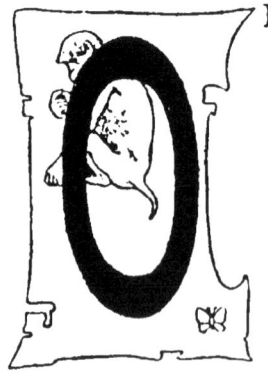ONCE upon a time, there lived in the mountains a Rabbit and a Monkey, who were great friends. One day, as they sat by the roadside hobnobbing together, who should come by but a man with a bamboo pole over his shoulder, and at each end of the pole was a bundle hung to a string; and there were plantains in one bundle, and sugar in the other.

Said the Monkey to the Rabbit, "Friend of my heart, do as I shall tell you. Go and sit upon the road in front of that man, and as soon as he sees you, run—he is sure to drop his load and follow. Then I will pick up his load, and hide it safely; and when you come back, we will share it together."

No sooner said than done: the Rabbit ran, and the man dropped his burden and ran after him; while the Monkey, who had been hiding in the tall grass by the wayside, pounced upon the sugar and the plantains, and climbed up into a tree, and began to gobble them up at his leisure.

By-and-by the man came back, hot and empty-handed, and finding that his goods were gone as well

The Rabbit and the Monkey

as the Rabbit, cursed loudly, and went home to be scolded by his wife.

Soon the Rabbit came back too, and began hunting about for his friend the Monkey. High and low he searched, and not a trace could he find; till he happened to cast his eyes aloft, and lo and behold, there was

Mr. Monkey up in a tree, munching away with every sign of enjoyment.

"Hullo, friend," said he, "come down out of that."

"I'm very comfortable here, thank you," said the Monkey.

"But where's my share?" asked the Rabbit indignantly.

"All gone, all gone," mumbled the Monkey, and pelted him with the plantain-peel and balls of paper made out of the packets where the sugar had been. "Why did you stay so long? I got hungry, and could not wait any longer."

The Rabbit thought his friend was joking, and would not believe it; but it was only too true—the greedy creature had not left a scrap.

"Do you really mean it?" said the poor Rabbit.

"If you don't believe me, come and see," said the Monkey, and seizing the Rabbit by his long ears, he hauled him up into the tree; and after mocking him, and making great game, he left him there, and went away.

Now the Rabbit was afraid to jump down from such a height, for fear of breaking his neck, so up in the tree he remained for a long time. Many animals passed under the tree, but none took pity on the rabbit, until at last came an old and foolish Rhinoceros, who rubbed his withered hide against the trunk.

"Kind Rhinoceros," said the Rabbit, "let me jump down upon your back."

The Rhinoceros, being a simple creature, agreed. Down came the Rabbit, with such a thud, that the Rhinoceros fell on his stupid old nose, and broke his fat old neck, and died.

The Rabbit ran away, and away he ran, until he came to the King's palace; and he hid under the King's golden throne. By-and-by in came the King, and in came the court; all the grandees stood around in their

The Rabbit and the Monkey

golden robes, glittering with rubies and diamonds, and their swords were girt about their waists. Suddenly they all heard a terrific sneeze!

Everybody said, "God bless you," while the King thundered out: "Who has the bad manners to sneeze in the King's presence?" Everybody looked at his neighbour, and wondered who did it. "Off with his head," shouted the King.

Another sneeze came. This time, however, everybody was on the watch, and they noticed that the sound came from under the King's golden throne. So they dived in, and lugged out the Rabbit, looking more dead than alive.

"All right," said the King, "off with his head." The executioner ran to get his sword.

But our friend the Rabbit, for all he was frightened, had his wits about him; and sitting up on his hind-legs, and putting his two fore-paws together, he said respectfully, "O great King, strike, but hear. If thou wilt send a score of men with me, I will give thee a dead Rhinoceros."

The King laughed, the courtiers laughed loud and long. However, just to see what would come of it, the King gave him a score of men.

The Rabbit led them to the place where the Rhinoceros fell on his stupid old nose, and there he lay dead. With great difficulty the men dragged the Rhinoceros home. They were very pleased to get a Rhinoceros, because his horn is good for curing many diseases, and the court physician ground his horn into powder, and made out of it a most wonderful medicine. And the King was so pleased, that he gave the Rabbit a fine new coat, and a horse to ride on.

So the Rabbit put on his fine coat, and got on the back of his horse, and rode off.

On the way, who should meet him but his friend the Monkey.

"Hullo!" says the Monkey, "where did you get all that finery?"

"The King gave it to me," says the Rabbit.

Says the Monkey, "And why should the King give all this to a fool like you?"

The Rabbit replied, "I, whom you call a fool, got it by sneezing under the King's golden throne; such a lucky sneeze, that the soothsayers prophesied to the King long life and many sons!" Then he rode away.

The Monkey fell a-thinking how nice it would be if he could get a fine coat and horse as the Rabbit had done. "I can sneeze," thought he; "what if I try my luck?"

So he scampered away, and away he scampered, till he came to the King's palace, and hid himself under the King's golden throne. When the King came in, and all his courtiers, in gorgeous array as before, our Monkey underneath the throne sneezed in the most auspicious manner he could contrive.

"Who is that?" thundered the King, glaring about him. "Who has the bad manners to sneeze in the King's presence?"

They searched about until they found the Monkey hidden under the throne, and hauled him out.

"What hast thou, wily tree-climber," asked the King,

The Rabbit and the Monkey

"that I should not bid the executioner cut off thy head?"

    The monkey had no answer ready. At last he
said, "O King, I have some plantain-
peel and pellets of paper." But
the King was angry at this,
and the greedy Monkey
was led away, and
his head was
cut off.

The Sparrow's Revenge

NCE there was a pair of Sparrows that were very fond of each other, and lived in a nest together as happy as the day was long. The hen laid eggs and sat upon them, and the cock went about picking up food for them both, and when he had got food enough, he sat on a twig close by the nest, and twittered for joy.

But it happened one day that a boy saw Cock Sparrow pecking at some seeds, and he picked up a stone and threw it at him, and killed him. So no food came home that morning, and Hen Sparrow grew anxious, and at last set out to find him.

In a little while she found his dead body lying in a ditch. She ruffled up her feathers and began to cry. "Who can have killed him?" she said; "my poor kind husband, who never did harm to any one." Then a Raven flew down from a tree, where he had been sitting, and told her how a cruel boy had thrown a stone at him and killed him for sport. He saw it, said the Raven, as he was sitting on the tree.

Now Hen Sparrow determined to have her revenge.

The Sparrow's Revenge

She was so much troubled that she left her eggs to hatch themselves, or to addle if they would; and gathering some straw, she plaited it into a beautiful straw carriage, with two old cotton-reels for wheels, and sticks for the shafts. Then she went to the hole of a Rat who was a friend of hers, and called down the hole, "Mr. Rat! Mr. Rat!"

"Yes, Mrs. Sparrow," said the Rat, coming out of the hole and making a polite bow.

"Some one has thrown a stone at my husband and killed him. Will you help me to get my revenge?"

"Why," said the Rat, "how can I help you?"

"By pulling me along in my carriage," said Mrs. Sparrow.

"Oh yes," said the Rat; "that I will." So he went down into his hole again, and washed his face, and combed his whiskers, and came up all spick and span.

Mrs. Sparrow tied the shafts of the straw carriage to the Rat, and Mrs. Sparrow got in, and off they went.

On the road they met a Scorpion. Said the Scorpion—

"Whither away, Mrs. Sparrow and Mr. Rat?"

Said the Hen Sparrow, "My friend Mr. Rat is pulling me along in my carriage of straw to punish a cruel boy who threw a stone at my husband and killed him."

"Quite right too," said the Scorpion. "May I come and help you? I have a beautiful sting in my tail."

"Oh, please do! come and get in," said the Sparrow.

In got the Scorpion, and away they went. By-and-by they saw a Snake.

"Good day, and God bless you," says the Snake. "Where are you going, may a mere reptile ask?"

"Mr. Scorpion and I are going to punish a cruel boy who threw a stone and killed my husband."

"Shall I come and help you?" asked the Snake. "I have fine teeth in my head to bite with."

"The more the merrier," replied Mrs. Sparrow. So in he got. They had not gone far before who should meet them but a Wolf.

"Hullo," says the Wolf gruffly; "where are you off to, I should like to know?"

"Mr. Rat is kind enough to draw me in my carriage, and we are all going to punish a cruel boy who threw a stone and killed my poor husband."

"May I come too?" growled the Wolf. "I can bite." He opened his big jaws and snarled.

"Oh, how kind you are!" said Mrs. Sparrow. "Do come! jump in, jump in!"

The poor Rat looked aghast at such a load to pull; but he was a gentlemanly Rat, and so, having offered to pull the carriage, he said nothing.

So the big Wolf got in, and nearly sat on the Scorpion's tail; if he had, he wouldn't have sat long, I think. However, the Scorpion got out of the way, and on they went all four, the poor Rat pulling with all his might, but rather slow at that.

In due time they arrived at the cruel boy's house. His mother was cooking the dinner, and his father was fast asleep in a chair. There was a river close by the house, and the Wolf went down to the river, and hid

The Sparrow's Revenge

himself there; the Snake crawled among the peats, and the Scorpion began to climb up into the chair where the man was sleeping.

Then Mrs. Hen Sparrow flew in at the door and twittered—

"Little boy! Little boy! There's a fish biting at your night-line!"

Up jumped the boy, and out he ran, to look at the night-line. But as he was stooping down and looking at the line to see if any fish were hooked, the Wolf pounced upon him, and bit him in the throat, and he died.

Then the cruel boy's mother went out to get some

peats, and as she put her hand in amongst them, the Snake bit her, and she gave a shriek and fell down and died. The shriek awoke her husband sleeping in his chair, and he began to get up, but by this time the Scorpion had climbed up the leg of the chair, so he stung the man, and the man died too.

Thus there was an end of the cruel boy who killed a harmless Sparrow for sport; and though his father and mother had done nothing, yet they ought not to have had a son so cruel, or, at least, they might have brought him up better. Anyhow, die they did, all three;
and Mrs. Hen Sparrow was so delighted that she
forgot all about her dead husband, and forgot
her eggs which were getting addled,
and went about chirruping until
she found another husband,
and made another nest,
and (I am sorry to
say) lived happily
ever after.

The Judgment of the Jackal

A MERCHANT was returning home from a long journey, riding upon a mule. As he drew near home, night overtook him; and he was forced to look out for shelter. Seeing a mill by the roadside, he knocked at the door.

"Come in!" said the Miller.

"May I stay here for the night?" asked the Merchant.

"By all means," said the Miller, "if you pay me well."

The Merchant thought this rather mean; because in those days a stranger was made welcome everywhere without paying anything. However, he made the best of it, and came in. The Miller led off his mule to the stable.

"Please take care of my mule," said the Merchant; "I have still a long way to go."

"Oh," said the Miller, "your mule will be all right." Then he rubbed him down and fed him.

22   The Judgment of the Jackal

In the morning the Merchant asked for his mule.

"The Merchant was much dismayed."

"I am very sorry," said the Miller; "he must have got loose last night, and I can't find him anywhere."

The Merchant was much dismayed. He went out to look for himself, and there, to be sure, was his mule, tied by the halter to the mill.

"Why, look here, Miller," says he, "here is the mule!"

"Oh no," says the Miller, "that mule is mine."

"Yours?" said the Merchant, getting angry. "Last night your stable was empty. And don't you think I know my own mule?"

"That is mine," said the Miller again; "my mill had a young mule in the night, and that is he."

The Merchant was now very angry indeed; but he could not help himself,

The Judgment of the Jackal 23

as he did not want to fight; he was a very peaceful Merchant. So he said—

"Well, I have no doubt it's all right; but just to satisfy me, let us ask the Rev. Dr. Jackal to decide between us; and whatever he says I will abide by."

"Very good," answered the Miller; and away they went to the den of his reverence the Jackal. Dr. Jackal

was sitting with his hind legs crossed, and smoking a hubble-bubble.

"Good morning, worthy gentlemen," said the Jackal; "how can I serve you?"

Said the Merchant, "Last night, my Lord Judge, I lodged with this Miller here, and he took charge of my mule; but now he says it has run away, though I saw it with my own eyes tied by the halter to his mill. He says that the mule I saw is his, and that his mill is the mother of it, and that it was born last night while I was asleep."

"Go back to the mill," said the Jackal, "and wait for me. I will just wash my face, and then I'll settle your business."

They went away, and waited a long time, but no Jackal. Late in the afternoon, they got tired of waiting for the Jackal, and determined to go and look for him. There he was still, sitting in his den and smoking a hubble-bubble.

"Why didn't you come?" asked the Miller. "We have been waiting for you all day."

"Oh, my dear sir, I was too busy," said the Jackal. "When I went to wash my face, I found that all the water had caught fire; I have only just put it out."

"You must be mad, your reverence," said the Miller. "Who ever heard of water catching fire?"

"And who ever heard," replied the Jackal, "of a mill having a young mule?"

The Miller saw that he was found out, and was so much ashamed that he gave back the mule to its owner, and the Merchant went home.

How the Mouse got into his Hole

A MERCHANT was going along the road one day with a sack of peas on the back of an Ox. The Ox was stung by a Fly, and gave a kick, and down fell the sack. A Mouse was passing by, and the Merchant said, "Mousie, if you will help me up with this sack I will give you a pea." The Mouse helped him up with the sack and got a pea for his trouble. He stole another, and a third he found on the road.

When he got home with his three peas he planted them in front of his hole. As he was planting them he said to them, "If you are not all three sprouting by to-morrow I'll cut you in pieces and give you to the black Ox." The peas were terribly frightened, and the next morning they had already begun to sprout, and each of them had two shoots. Then he said, "If I don't find you in blossom to-morrow I'll cut you in pieces and give you to the black Ox." When he went to look next day they were all in blossom. So he said, "If I don't find ripe peas on you to-morrow I'll cut you in pieces and give you to the black Ox." Next day they had pods full of ripe peas on them.

So every day he used to eat lots of peas, and in this manner he got very fat. One day a pretty young lady Mouse came to see him.

"Good morning, Sleekie," said she; "how are you?"

"Good morning, Squeakie," said he; "I'm quite well, thank you."

"Why, Sleekie," said she, "how fat you are."

"Am I?" said he. "I suppose that's because I have plenty to eat."

"What do you eat, Sleekie?" asked the pretty young lady Mouse.

"Peas, Squeakie," said the other.

"Where do you get them, Sleekie?"

"They grow all of themselves in my garden, Squeakie."

"Will you give me some, please?" asked the lady Mouse.

"Oh yes, if you will stay in my garden, you may have as many as you like."

So Squeakie stayed in Sleekie's garden, and they both ate so many peas that they got fatter and fatter every day.

One day Squeakie said to Sleekie, "Let's try which can get into the hole quickest." Squeakie was slim, and she had not been at the peas so long as Sleekie, so she got into the hole easily enough; but Sleekie was so fat that he could not get in at all.

He was very much frightened, and went off in hot

The Mouse in his Hole

haste to the Carpenter, and said to him, "Carpenter, please pare off a little flesh from my ribs, so that I can get into my hole."

"Do you think I have nothing better to do than paring down your ribs?" said the Carpenter angrily, and went on with his work.

The Mouse went to the King, and said, "O King, I can't get into my hole, and the Carpenter will not pare down my ribs; will you make him do it?"

"Get out," said the King; "do you think I have nothing better to do than look after your ribs?"

So the Mouse went to the Queen. Said he, "Queen, I can't get into my hole, and the King won't tell the Carpenter to pare down my ribs. Please divorce him."

"Bother you and your ribs," said the Queen; "I am not going to divorce my husband because you have made yourself fat by eating too much."

The Mouse went to the Snake. "Snake, bite the Queen, and tell her to divorce the King, because he will not tell the Carpenter to pare my ribs down and let me get into my hole."

"Get away," said the Snake; "or I'll swallow you up, ribs and all; the fatter you are, the better I shall be pleased."

He went to the Stick, and said, "Stick, beat the Snake, because she won't bite the Queen, who won't divorce the King and make him tell the Carpenter to pare down my ribs, and let me get into my hole."

"Off with you," said the Stick; "I'm sleepy, because I have just beaten a thief; I can't be worried about your ribs."

He went to the Furnace, and said, "Furnace, burn

the Stick, and make it beat the Snake, that he may bite the Queen and make her divorce the King, who won't tell the Carpenter to pare down my ribs, and let me get into my hole."

"Get along with you," said the Furnace; "I am cooking the King's dinner, and I have no time now to see about your ribs."

He went to the Ocean, and said, "Ocean, put out the Fire, and make it burn the Stick, so that it may beat the Snake, and the Snake may bite the Queen, and she may divorce the King, who won't tell the Carpenter to pare down my ribs, and let me get into my hole."

"Don't bother me," said the Ocean; "it's high tide, and all the fishes are jumping about, and giving me no rest."

He went to the Elephant, and said, "O Elephant, drink up the Ocean, that it may put out the Fire, and the Fire may burn the Stick, and the Stick may beat the Snake, and the Snake may bite the Queen, and the Queen may divorce the King, and make him tell the Carpenter to pare down my ribs, and let me get into my hole."

"Go away, little Mouse," said the Elephant; "I have just drunk up a whole lake, and I really can't drink any more."

He went to the Creeper, and said, "Dear Creeper, do please choke the Elephant, that he may drink up the Ocean, and the Ocean may put out the Fire, and the Fire may burn the Stick, and the Stick may beat the Snake, and the Snake may bite the Queen, and the Queen may divorce the King, and the King may tell the Carpenter to pare down my ribs, and let me get into my hole."

"Not I," says the Creeper; "I am stuck fast here to this tree, and I couldn't get away to please a fat little Mouse."

Then he went to the Scythe, and said, "Scythe, please cut loose the Creeper, that it may choke the Elephant, and the Elephant may drink up the Ocean, and the Ocean may put out the Fire, and the Fire may burn the Stick, and the Stick may beat the Snake, and the Snake may bite the Queen, and the Queen may divorce the King, and the King may tell the Carpenter to pare down my ribs, and let me get into my hole."

"With pleasure," said the Scythe, who is always sharp.

So the Scythe cut the Creeper loose, and the Creeper began to choke the Elephant, and the Elephant ran off and began to drink up the Ocean, and the Ocean began to put out the Fire, and the Fire began to burn the Stick, and the Stick began to beat the Snake, and the Snake began to bite the Queen, and the Queen told the King she was going to divorce him, and the King was frightened, and ordered the Carpenter to pare Sleekie's ribs, and at last Sleekie got into his hole.

D

King Solomon and the Owl

ONCE King Solomon was hunting all alone in the forest. Night fell, and King Solomon lay down under a tree to sleep. Over his head, on the branch of a tree, sat a huge Owl; and the Owl hooted so loud and so long, Too-whit too-woo! Too-whit too-woo! that Solomon could not sleep. Solomon looked up at the Owl, and said—

"Tell me, O Owl, why do you hoot all night long upon the trees?"

Said the Owl—

> "I hoot to waken those that sleep,
> As soon as day's first beams do peep;
> That they may rise, and say their prayers,
> And not be caught in this world's cares."

Then he went on again, Too-whit! too-woo! shaking his solemn old head to and fro. He was a melancholy Owl; I think he must have been crossed in love.

Solomon thought this Owl very clever to roll out beautiful poetry like that, off-hand as it were. He asked the Owl again—

"Tell me, O wise Owl, why do you shake your very solemn old head?"

King Solomon and the Owl

Said the Owl—

> "I shake my head, to let all know
> This world is but a fleeting show.
> Men's days are flying with quick wings;
> So take no joy in earthly things.
>
> "Yet men will fix their hearts below
> Upon the pleasures that must go.
> Their joy is gone when they are dead;
> And that is why I shake my head."

This touched King Solomon in a tender place, for he was himself rather fond of earthly delights. He sighed, and asked again—

"O most ancient and wise Owl! tell me why you never eat grain?"

Answered the Owl—

> "The bearded grain I do not eat,
> Because, when Adam ate some wheat,
> He was turned out of Paradise:
> So Adam's sin has made me wise.
>
> "If I should eat a single grain,
> The joys of heaven I should not gain.
> And so, to keep my erring feet,
> The bearded grain I never eat."

Thought Solomon to himself, "I don't remember reading that story in Genesis, but perhaps he is right. I must look it up when I get home." Then he spoke to the Owl once more, and said—

"And now, good Owl, tell me why you drink no water at night?"

Said the Owl—

> "Since water all the world did drown
> In Noah's day, I will drink none.
> Were I to drink a single drop,
> My life would then most likely stop."

King Solomon and the Owl

Solomon was delighted to find the Owl so wise. "O my Owl," said he, "all my life long I have been looking for a counsellor who had reasons to give for what he did; I have never found one until I found you. Now I beg you to come home with me to-morrow, and you shall be my chief counsellor, and whatever I purpose I will first ask your advice."

The Owl was equally delighted, and said, "Thank you." Thinking of the greatness that was to be his, the Owl stopped crying Too-whit! too-woo! and Solomon went to sleep.

The Camel's Neck

ONCE upon a time there was a very religious Camel; at least, he was religious after the fashion of his country, that is, he used to mortify his flesh by fasting, and scratch himself with thorns, and lie awake all night meditating upon the emptiness of the world. That is what men used to do in that country, in order to please their gods. One of these gods was very much pleased with the piety of the Camel; so one night, as the Camel was fasting, and saying over and over to himself, "Vanity of vanities, all is vanity," the god

33

appeared before him. He was a curious-looking god, and he had four hands instead of two; but the Camel did not mind that, nor did he laugh; on the contrary, he went down on his knees and bowed before him.

"O Camel," said this god, "I have seen your fasting and heard your prayers; and I have come to reward you. Choose what boon you like, and it shall be yours."

"O mighty god, I should like to have a neck eight miles long."

The god answered, "Be it so!" and immediately the Camel felt his neck shooting out like a telescope, until it was eight miles long. It shot out so fast, that the Camel found it hard to escape running his head against the trees. However, he steered it successfully, barring a bump or two; and as by the time his neck stopped growing he was far out of sight of the god, he could not even say thank you.

Now perhaps you will wonder why this Camel wanted a neck so long as eight miles? I will tell you. The reason was, that for all his fastings and penances, he was a lazy Camel, and he wanted to graze without the trouble of walking about. And now he could easily graze for a distance of eight miles all round in a circle, without moving from the spot where he lay. But it was rather dangerous, though he thought nothing of that; for when his head was grazing a few miles away, the hunters might stick a spear into his body, or tie his legs together, without his seeing them.

All the summer the Camel had a fine time of it; he lay still and comfortable and sent his head foraging around, and strange to say, no harm happened to him. But before long the rainy season began. In the rainy season there are storms every day, and it rains cats and

The Camel's Neck

dogs. So when the rain began, the Camel wanted to keep dry, but he could not at first find a shed or a shelter eight miles long, or anything like it. At last he lit on a long winding cave that held most of his long neck. So he ran his neck into the cave, and lay still, with the rain pouring upon his body.

This was bad enough, but worse was to come. For it happened that in this cave lived a He-jackal and a She-jackal.

When the Jackals saw this extraordinary neck winding along their cave, they were frightened, and hid away.

"What is this snake?" said the He-jackal to his wife.

"Oh dear, I don't know!" whimpered his wife, "I never saw a snake like this."

They kept quiet, the head passed out of view into the inner part of the cave; then after a while, the creature lay still.

"Let us smell him!" said the He-jackal.

They smelt him. "He smells nice," said the She-jackal; "not a bit like a snake."

"Let us taste him!" said the He-jackal.

They took a bite; the Camel stirred restlessly. They took another bite, and liked that better still. They went on biting. The Camel curled round his head to see what was going on; but before the Camel's head could get back more than a mile or two, he grew so weak from loss of blood, that he could move no more, and he died.

So died the idle Camel, because the god granted him his foolish wish. Perhaps our wishes are often just as foolish, if we only knew it; and perhaps if they were fulfilled they would be the bane of us, as happened to the lazy and religious Camel.

The Quail and the Fowler

A FOWLER once caught a Quail. Said the Quail to the Fowler—

"O Fowler, I know four things that will be useful for you to know."

"What are they?" asked the Fowler.

"Well," said the Quail, "I don't mind telling you three of them now. The first is: Fast caught, fast keep; never let a thing go when once you have got it. The second is: He is a fool that believes everything he hears. And the third is this: It's of no use crying over spilt milk."

The Quail and the Fowler

The Fowler thought these very sensible maxims. "And what is the fourth?" he asked.

"Ah," said the Quail, "you must set me free if you want to hear the fourth."

The Fowler, who was a simple fellow, set the Quail free. The Quail fluttered up into a tree, and said—

"I see you take no notice of what I tell you. Fast caught, fast keep, I said; and yet you have let me go."

"Why, so I have," said the Fowler, and scratched his head. He was a foolish Fowler, I think. "Well, never mind; what is the fourth thing? You promised to tell me, and I am sure an honourable Quail will never break his word."

"The fourth thing I have to tell you is this: In my inside is a beautiful diamond, weighing ten pounds. And if you had not let me go, you would have had that diamond, and you need never have done any more work in all your life."

"Oh dear, oh dear, what a fool I am!" cried the Fowler. He fell on his face, and clutched at the grass, and began to cry.

"Ha, ha, ha!" laughed the Quail. "He is a fool who believes everything he hears."

"Eh? what?" said the Fowler, and stopped crying.

"Do you think a little carcase like mine can hold a diamond as big as your head?" asked the Quail, roaring with laughter. "And even if it were true, where's the use of crying over spilt milk?"

The Quail spread his wings. "Good-bye," said he; "better luck next time, Fowler." And he flew away.

The Fowler sat up. "Well," said he, "that's true, sure enough." He got up and brushed the mud off his clothes. "If I have lost a Quail," said he, "I've learnt something." And he went home, a sadder but a wiser man.

The King of the Kites

A MOUSE one day met a Frog, whom he knew very well; but the Frog turned up his flat nose, and would not speak to him.

"Friend Frog," said the Mouse, "why are you so proud to-day?"

"Because I am King of the Kites," said Froggie.

You must not suppose that this means a paper kite with a tail. There is a kind of bird called a Kite; it is like a Hawk, only bigger. How absurd it was of this Frog, who could not even fly, to call himself the King of the Kites! And the Mouse was just as absurd, for he answered—

"Stuff and nonsense! I am King of the Kites!"

I don't know whether they really believed this themselves, or whether they were only trying to show off. Anyhow, both stuck to it stoutly, and a pretty quarrel was the result. The Mouse grew red in the face; and as for Froggie, he was nearly bursting with rage.

At last they agreed to refer the decision to a council. The council was made up of a Bat, a Squirrel, and a Parrot. The Parrot took the chair, because he was the biggest, and also because he could talk most, and was therefore thought to be wise.

"I vote for the Mouse," said the Bat; not that he knew anything about it, but you see a Bat is very like a Mouse, and he wanted to stand up for the family.

"And I," said the Squirrel, "vote for my friend Froggie." He knew nothing about it either, but he wanted to show that even a Squirrel has an opinion of his own.

So it fell to the Parrot to give the casting vote, and decide the matter. He took a long time to decide, about two hours; and while he was thinking, and the others were all intent to hear what he should say, down from the sky swooped a Kite; and the Kite stuck one claw into the Mouse's back, and one claw into the Frog, and carried them both away to his nest, and ate them for dinner.

So that was the end of the two Kings of the Kites.
The other three creatures, in a great fright,
made themselves scarce, lest the
Kite should come back and
eat them too.

The Jackal and the Camel

ONCE a Camel was grazing in a forest. He had a ring in his nose, as the custom is, and to the ring was tied a string, by which the Camel's master used to lead him about. As the Camel grazed, this leading-string became entangled in a bush, and the Camel could not get it loose. This misfortune so much confused the mind of the Camel that he did not know what to do.

Suddenly, as the Camel was struggling to get free from the bush, a Jackal appeared.

"Brother Jackal," said the Camel, "do please set me free from this bush."

"Brother Camel," said the Jackal, "I will set you free, only you must pay me for it. Do not the wise say, ' Even a brother will not serve thee for nothing ' ?"

"What shall I pay you, brother Jackal? I am a very poor Camel."

"You shall pay me," quoth the Jackal, "a pound of your flesh."

This was a hard condition, but there was nothing for it. "Better to lose a pound of my flesh," thought the

The Jackal and the Camel

Camel, "than lose my life." So he agreed to pay the Jackal a pound of flesh.

Then the Jackal set the Camel free, and the Camel sat down on the ground and said—

"I am ready; take your pound of flesh."

"Open your mouth, then," said the Jackal.

"Why?" asked the Camel.

"Because I choose to take my pound of flesh from your tongue."

This was a terrible blow. The Camel could not agree, because he knew that if his tongue were torn out, he was bound to die.

So he said, "I did not promise you my tongue."

"You did," said the Jackal.

"Don't tell lies," said the Camel; "where are your witnesses?"

Away trotted the Jackal to find a witness. First he asked the Lion if he would bear witness that he heard the Camel promise to give his tongue. He promised to give him the half of all he should get, as a reward.

"Go away," said the King of Beasts; "I am a Lion, not a liar."

Then he asked the Tiger, but the Tiger said—

"I don't care for Camel's meat, so it isn't worth my while."

And so the Jackal tried one beast after another, but none of them would help him, until he came to the Wolf.

"Friend Wolf," said the Jackal, "if you will only swear that you heard the Camel promise me his tongue, you shall have half."

"Half a tongue?" quoth the Wolf; "that's poor provender."

"No, no," said the Jackal, "half the Camel. Don't you see that if we tear out his tongue, the Camel will soon bleed to death."

"True, so he will," said the Wolf. "Well, I agree."

So the Wolf and the Jackal went back to the Camel, and the Wolf said, raising his right forepaw to heaven—

"I swear by heaven that I heard this Camel promise to give his tongue to this Jackal."

Of course this was a lie, and they all knew it; but the Camel did not like to appear mean, and besides, they were two to one.

"Very well," said the Camel; "come and take it." The Camel opened his mouth wide. The Jackal put his head in the Camel's mouth, and as he did so, the Camel curled his tongue backward, so that the Jackal could not reach it.

The Jackal pulled his head out again, and said to the Wolf—

"My mouth is too small, you try now—you have a big gape."

Then the Wolf put his head in the Camel's mouth. The Camel curled his tongue back and back, and the Wolf pushed in his head further and further; at last all the Wolf's head was inside. Then the Camel snapped his jaws together upon the Wolf's neck.

"O Daddy Camel," said the Wolf, half throttled; "what is this?"

"This," said the Jackal, rolling up the whites of his eyes to the sky in a most pious fashion; "this is the result of telling a lie." The Camel said nothing at all, but simply throttled the Wolf to death, and the Jackal ran away.

I think you will agree with me, that the Jackal, who made the Wolf tell a lie, was wickeder than the Wolf who told it; but yet he laughed at the Wolf, and got off himself scot-free. That often happens in this world; but we will hope that some other time his sin was bound to find him out.

The Wise Old Shepherd

ONCE upon a time, a snake went out of his hole to take an airing. He crawled about, greatly enjoying the scenery and the fresh whiff of the breeze, until, seeing an open door, he went in. Now this door was the door of the palace of the King, and inside was the King himself, with all his courtiers.

Imagine their horror at seeing a huge Snake crawling in at the door. They all ran away except the King, who felt that his rank forbade him to be a coward, and the King's son. The King called out for somebody to come and kill the Snake; but this horrified them still more, because in that country the people believed it to be wicked to kill any living thing, even snakes, and scorpions, and wasps. So the courtiers did nothing, but the young Prince obeyed his father, and killed the Snake with his stick.

After a while the Snake's wife became anxious, and set out in search of her husband. She too saw the open door of the palace, and in she went. O horror! there on the floor lay the body of her husband, all covered with blood, and quite dead. No one saw the Snake's wife crawl in; she inquired from a white ant what had happened, and when she found that the young Prince had killed her husband, she made a vow, that as he had made her a widow, so she would make his wife a widow.

That night, while all the world was asleep, the Snake crept into the Prince's bedroom, and coiled around his neck. The Prince slept on, and when he awoke in the morning, he was surprised to find his neck encircled with the coils of a Snake. He was afraid to stir, so there he remained, until the Prince's mother became anxious, and went to see what was the matter. When she entered his room, and saw him in this plight, she gave a loud shriek, and ran off to tell the King.

"Call the archers," said the King. The archers came, and the King told them to go into the Prince's room, and shoot the Snake that was coiled about his neck. They were so clever, that they could easily do this without hurting the Prince at all.

In came the archers in a row, fitted the arrows to the bows, the bows were raised ready to shoot, when, on a sudden, from the Snake there issued a voice, which spoke as follows :—

"O archers! wait, and hear me before you shoot. It is not fair to carry out the sentence before you have heard the case. Is not this good law, an eye for an eye, and a tooth for a tooth? Is it not so, O King?"

"Yes," replied the King, "that is our law."

"Then," said the Snake, "I plead the law. Your son has made me a widow, so it is fair and right that I should make his wife a widow."

The Wise Old Shepherd

"That sounds right enough," said the King, "but right and law are not always the same thing. We had better ask somebody who knows."

They asked all the judges, but none of them could tell the law of the matter. They shook their heads, and said they would look up all their law-books, and see whether anything of the sort had ever happened before, and if so, how it had been decided. That is the way judges used to decide cases in that country, though I daresay it sounds to you a very funny way. It looked as if they had not much sense in their own heads, and perhaps that was true. The upshot of all was, that not a judge would give any opinion; so the King sent messengers all over the country-side, to see if they could find somebody somewhere who knew something.

One of these messengers found a party of five Shepherds, who were sitting upon a hill and trying to decide a quarrel of their own. They gave their opinions so freely, and in language so very strong, that the King's messenger said to himself, "Here are the men for us. Here are five men, each with an opinion of his own, and all different." Post-haste he scurried back to the King, and told him he had found at last some one ready to judge the knotty point.

So the King and the Queen, and the Prince and the Princess, and all the courtiers, got on horseback, and away they galloped to the hill whereupon the five Shepherds were sitting, and the Snake too went with them, coiled round the neck of the Prince.

When they got to the Shepherds' hill, the Shepherds were dreadfully frightened. At first they thought that the strangers were a gang of robbers; and when they saw that it was the King, their next thought was that one of their misdeeds had been found out, and each of them began thinking what was the last thing he had done, and wondering, was it that? But the King and his Court got off their horses, and said good-day in the most civil way. So the Shepherds felt their minds set at ease again. Then the King said—

"Worthy Shepherds, we have a question to put to you, which not all the judges in all the courts of my city have been able to solve. Here is my son, and here, as you see, is a Snake coiled round his neck. Now, the husband of this Snake came creeping into my palace hall, and my son the Prince killed him; so this Snake, who is the wife of the other, says that as my son has made her a widow, so she has a right to widow my son's wife. What do you think about it?"

The first Shepherd said, "I think she is quite right, my lord King. If any one made my wife a widow, I would pretty soon do the same to him."

This was brave language, and the other Shepherds shook their heads and looked fierce. But the King was puzzled, and could not quite understand it. You see, in the first place, if the man's wife were a widow, the man would be dead; and then it is hard to see how he could do anything. So to make sure, the King asked the second Shepherd whether that was his opinion too?

"Yes," said the second Shepherd; "now the Prince has killed the Snake, the Snake has a right to kill the Prince, if he can."

But that was not of much use either, as the Snake was as dead as a door-nail. So the King passed on to the third.

The Wise Old Shepherd

"I agree with my mates," said the third Shepherd, "because, you see, a Prince is a Prince, but then a Snake is a Snake."

That was quite true, they all admitted; but it did not seem to help the matter much. Then the King asked the fourth Shepherd to say what he thought.

The fourth Shepherd said, "An eye for an eye, and a tooth for a tooth; so I think a widow should be a widow, if so be she don't marry again."

By this time the poor King was so puzzled that he hardly knew whether he stood on his head or his heels. But there was still the fifth Shepherd left, the oldest and wisest of them all; and the fifth Shepherd said—

"O King, I should like to ask two questions."

"Ask twenty, if you like," said the King. He did not promise to answer them, so he could afford to be generous.

"First, I ask the Princess how many sons she has?"

"Four," said the Princess.

"And how many sons has Mistress Snake here?"

"Seven," said the Snake.

"Then," said the old Shepherd, "it will be quite fair for Mistress Snake to kill his Highness the Prince, when her Highness the Princess has had three sons more."

"I never thought of that," said the Snake. "Good-bye, King, and all you good people. Send a message when the Princess has had three more sons, and you may count upon me—I will not fail you." So saying, she uncoiled from the Prince's neck and slid away among the grass.

    The King and the Prince and everybody shook hands
with the wise old Shepherd, and went home
again. And as the Princess never had any
more sons at all, she and the Prince
lived happily for many years;
and if they are not dead
they are living
still.

Beware of Bad Company

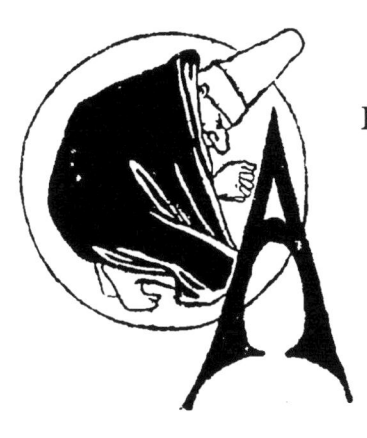

A BEAUTIFUL young Swan lived by a beautiful lake. All day long he used to sail gracefully over the water, curving his neck to look at his own image, or pluming his white wings; and when he was tired, he would go to his nest in the rushes, and sleep, or play with his brothers and sisters.

In a tree above that lake was a Crow. You know that Crows are dirty birds, and they feed on offal and refuse, and people dislike them; but the Swan was white and clean. Still, strange as it may seem, this Swan struck up a fast friendship with the Crow. His mother and father begged him to keep out of bad company, but he would not listen to them. He had done better to keep to his own kind, but wilful will have his way, and the Swan was sorry for it too late.

One day the Crow said to his friend the Swan, "Come, old boy, let us go and have some fun."

"I'm your Swan," says the other, and away they flew.

They came to a tree, and under the tree was a very pious man, saying his prayers.

"Here's a joke," said the Crow. "Now we shall see sport."

He picked up a lump of mud from the ground, and flew up into the tree, and then he dropped the mud, splash, on the pious man's head.

This interrupted his prayers, and he could not help feeling angry, although he was so pious. So up got he, and looked about to see who had done the mischief.

By this time the mischievous Crow had flown off, and he was caw-caw-cawing on another tree, out of reach. But the Swan sat still: he was not learned in mischief, and he did not know what to do. Then the pious man looked up into the tree, and saw the Swan sitting there, so of course he thought it was the Swan who had dropped a piece of mud on his head. He had a big catapult with him, so he put a stone in his catapult, and slick! he shot the Swan.

Down fell the Swan with a great thud. He felt that his end was near, and how sorry he was now that he had had anything to do with the bad Crow. However, it was too late now to be sorry, so he began to sing. They say that Swans never sing in all their life, but when they are about to die they sing beautifully; and this is what the Swan sang to the pious man:—

> "I am no Crow, as you must know,
>   But a Swan that lived by a lovely lake;
> With bad companions I would go,
>   And now I die for a bad friend's sake."

Then the Swan died, and the pious man finished his prayers.

The Foolish Wolf

A WOLF and an Ass were great friends, and they spent most of their time playing at an original game of their own. The game was easy enough to learn; you could play it yourselves; and it was this. First the Ass used to run away from the Wolf as hard as he could, and the Wolf used to follow; and then the Wolf would run as hard as he could from the Ass, and the Ass would follow.

One day, as the Wolf was running away full tilt from the Ass, a Boy saw them.

"Ha, ha, ha," said the Boy, "what a coward that Wolf is, to run away from an Ass." He thought, you see, that the Wolf was afraid of being eaten by the Ass.

The Wolf heard him, and was very angry. He stopped short, and said to the Boy—

"So you think I am a coward, little Boy? You shall rue the word. I'm brave enough to eat you, as you shall find out this very night; for I will come and carry you off from your home."

If the Wolf was no coward, at least he was a foolish

Wolf to tell the Boy if he meant to carry him off, as I think you will agree with me.

The Boy went home to tell his mother. "Mother," said he, "a Wolf is coming to-night to carry me off."

"Oh, never mind if he does," said the Boy's mother, "he won't hurt you."

The Boy did not feel quite so sure about that, for he had seen sharp teeth in the mouth of the Wolf. So he chose out a big and sharp stone, and put it in his pocket. Why he did not hide, I can't tell you, for he never told me; but my private opinion is, he was almost as foolish as the Wolf.

Well, when night came, the Boy's mother went to bed, and she was soon snoring, but the Boy stayed up to wait for the Wolf. About ten o'clock came a knock at the door.

"Come in," said the Boy.

The Wolf opened the door, and came in, and says he, "Now, Boy, you must come along with me."

"All right," says the Boy, "mother doesn't mind."

I have never been able to understand why his mother did not mind, but perhaps he was a very naughty Boy, and she was glad to get rid of him. If he did nothing but pull his sisters' hair, and put spiders down their necks, he was just as well out of the house, I think.

So the Boy got on the Wolf's back, and the Wolf trotted off briskly to his den. Then the Wolf thought to himself, "I have had my dinner, and I don't want any Boy to-night. Suppose I leave him for to-morrow, and go for a spin with my friend the Jackass."

So he left the Boy in his den, and off he went after the Jackass.

The Foolish Wolf

What makes me think more than ever that he was a foolish Wolf, is that he never even tied the Boy's legs together. So when the Wolf was gone, the Boy went out of the den, and climbed up a tree.

In an hour or two back came the Wolf, ready for bed. He looked in at the mouth of the den, but no Boy.

"Where on earth has that Boy got to?" said he; "I left him here safe and sound." It never occurred to this Wolf that legs can walk, and Boys can climb trees. He felt very anxious, and as many people do when their wits are puzzled, he opened his mouth wide.

The Boy saw him standing at the opening of the den, with his mouth wide open, so he pulled the sharp stone out of his pocket, and threw it in. This Boy was a very good shot with a stone, and the stone went straight into the Wolf's inside, and cut his inside so much that he died.

Then the Boy climbed down from the tree, and
   he was at home in time for breakfast. I don't
     know whether his mother was pleased
        to see him or not; but there he was,
         and there he stayed, and if he
           has not gone away, he is
             there still.

Reflected Glory

THERE was a Shepherd who owned a multitude of goats. Among these was one Goat, weak and lame. You might suppose that the shepherd took especial care of this lame Goat, but not he; on the contrary, he beat him and bullied him, and made his whole life a misery.

A time came when the lame Goat could stand it no longer. So watching his chance, he gave his master the slip, and into the forest and far away. As he hobbled along, he trembled to think of the ferocious beasts that the forest was full of; but even to be devoured by an evil beast was better far than to be for ever beaten.

The lame Goat made up his mind that the only way by which he could save his life was to gain the protection of some powerful beast. So he kept his eyes open as he hobbled along; and, by-and-by, what should he see but a dark cave, and at the mouth of the cave, a Lion's footprints. Now a Lion was just the beast the Goat wanted, for to begin with, he is the King of Beasts, and all the other beasts fear him; and then, too, he is a noble beast, and if he passes his word he will never break it. Of course, it might be that the Lion would eat our Goat first, and ask questions afterwards; but the Goat had to take his chance of that.

The upshot of it was, that the lame Goat sat down by the Lion's den, and waited.

By-and-by, trippity trip, trippity trip, and up came a Jackal. Said the Jackal to the Goat, "God bless you, Gaffer Goat, you'll be the first food that has passed my lips this many a day."

"Dear grandson," said the Goat, "God bless you too. I'm here to be eaten, that is true enough; but I'm meat for your betters. He whose footprints you see here has bidden me wait until he wants me."

The Jackal looked at the footprints, and saw they were a Lion's. "Aha," thought he, "let sleeping dogs lie. If I eat the Lion's meat, the Lion will devour my cubs." Then he went away sorrowful.

A little while, and trappity trap, trappity trap, up came a Wolf. Quoth the Wolf—

"Well met, Nuncle Goat; you make my mouth water. A five days' fast is sauce for the dinner."

"Well met, my dear nephew," says the lame Goat. "But you had better leave me alone. I'm food for your betters. Look upon these footprints, and let me tell you that he who made them has bidden me wait here until he is hungry."

"Oho," said the Wolf, "a Lion. Who tackles the strong will not live long. If I eat King Lion's meat, King Lion will make a meal of my cubs." Away went the Wolf, trappity trap, trappity-trap.

A little while more, and swish, swish, swish, the Lion himself came stalking slowly along, whisking away the flies with his tail. When he saw the Goat sitting beside his den, says he—

"Friend Goat, what want you here? Are you anxious to make a meal for me?"

"O King Lion," said the Goat, bowing before him very humbly, "here I have been sitting these two hours, and wolves and jackals came to eat me; but the sight of your footprints was safety for me: I told them I was yours, and they took to their heels for fear. Now eat me if you will; for yours I am."

Then the Lion said, "O Goat, if you have called yourself mine, never will I devour you. I will see to it that you are well treated."

Then the Lion went out and found an Elephant, who greeted him with the greatest respect. "Elephant," said the Lion, "I want you to do something for me."

"Speak on," said the Elephant, "do it I will."

The Lion said, "There is a poor lame Goat has thrown himself on my mercy, and I have thought of a plan by which he can be fed. If you will suffer him to mount on your back, then while you go grazing about, he can browse upon the young shoots of the trees as you pass under."

"That is a good idea," said the Elephant, "and I'll do it for you willingly, and indeed anything else in my power."

If the Lion was pleased at the kindness of the Elephant, more pleased was the lame Goat; and a happy life was his from that day. Never again was he
  beaten by a cruel goatherd: but he fed on the fat
    of the land, and lived to a green old age; and
      I hope we may be half as happy as he was.

The Cat and the Sparrows

THERE was once a pair of Sparrows that lived in a tree. They used to hop about all over the place, picking up seeds or anything they could find to eat. One day, when they came back with their pickings, the Cock had found some rice, and the Hen a few lentils. They put it all in an earthen pot, and then proceeded to cook their dinner. Then they divided the mess into two equal parts.

The Cock was rather greedy, so he would not wait while his wife put out the fire and got ready to join in the meal. No! he gobbled up his share at once, before she could begin.

When at last the poor Hen came up, her greedy mate would not let her rest even then. "Go and get me a drink of water," said he quite rudely.

She was a very kind wife, so without taking any notice of his rudeness, off she went for the water.

While she was gone the Cock-sparrow's eyes fell on his wife's share of the dinner. "Ah," thought he, "how I should like another bit! Well, why shouldn't I have it? A man does all the work, and women don't want much to eat at any time." So without any more ado, he just set to, and gobbled up his wife's share.

Back came the Hen-sparrow with a drink of water for her husband. When he had drunk it up (and I am afraid he forgot to say thank you), she turned round to look for her dinner. Lo and behold! there was none. What could have become of it? As she was wondering, she happened to look at her husband; he looked so guilty that there could be no manner of doubt where her dinner was.

"You greedy bird," said she, "why have you eaten my dinner?"

"I haven't touched your dinner," said the Cock angrily.

"I'm sure you have," said she, "or you would not look so guilty. Why, you are actually blushing." And so indeed he was; the tip of his beak was quite red.

However, he still denied it, and grew angrier and angrier, as people do when they know they are in the wrong. They had a terrible quarrel. At last the Hen-sparrow said, "Well, I know a way to find out whether you are telling lies or not. You come along with me." And she made him go with her to the well.

Across the top of the well she stretched a piece of string, and she sat on the middle of the string, and began to chirp, "If I am telling lies, I pray I may fall in." But though she sat there a long time, chirping away, she did not fall in.

Then came the Cock-sparrow's turn. He perched on the string and began to chirrup, "If I am telling lies, may I fall into the well;" but hardly had he got the

The Cat and the Sparrows

words out of his mouth, when —splash! down he went.

Then the Hen was very sorry that she had proposed this plan; she began to weep and cheep, and said—"Alas, alas, why didn't I leave it alone? What does it matter if he eats my dinner, so long as I have my dear husband? Now I have killed him by my folly."

Just at that moment up came a Cat.

"What's the matter?" said the Cat.

"Cheep, cheep, cheep," went the Hen-sparrow. "My husband has fallen into the well, and I don't know how to get him out."

"If I get him out," said the Cat, "will you let me eat him?"

"Of course you may," said the Hen-sparrow.

So the Cat climbed down, and pulled out the Cock-sparrow. When she had brought him to the edge of the well, said she, "Now I'm going to eat him as you promised."

"Oh, all right," said the Hen. "But stop a minute, your mouth is dirty. I am sure you have been eating mice. Now haven't you?"

"Why, yes," said the Cat, "so I have."

"Well," said the Hen-sparrow, "you must get yourself clean. We birds are clean creatures, and you must positively wash your mouth before you begin."

Away went the Cat, and washed her mouth clean, and came back again.

The Hen-sparrow looked at her carefully. "You have not washed your whiskers," said she; "they are still dirty."

The Cat went obediently and washed her whiskers.

Meanwhile the Cock-sparrow had been sitting on the edge of the well in the sun, and by this time his feathers were quite dry. So his Hen chirped to him, "Now, dear, you can fly, let's be off." And off they flew together, and the Cat was left licking her chops and wishing she had not been such a fool.

The Foolish Fish

A FISH was once flapping and flopping on the sand by the banks of a river. She was a lady Fish—how she got there I don't know; but she had been better to stay at home, as you shall hear. Well, she flapped away on the sand, and couldn't get off; she began to feel very dry. A man came by, riding upon a horse. "O Man," shouted the Fish, "do carry me back to the water again, or I shall be dried up and die."

"No, no," said the Man, "not I, indeed! You are a she, and I have had so much bother with shes in my life that I shall keep clear of you."

"O dear good Man!" cried the Fish, "do please help me, and I will promise not to behave badly; I'll be as nice as any man could be. Just think! if you leave me here, I shall dry into a stick, or somebody will come along and eat me."

The Man scratched his head, and wondered what he ought to do; but at last he took pity on the Fish, and got down off his horse. Then he picked up the Fish and put her on his shoulder, and walked down to the water. "Now then," said he, "in with you."

"Take me into deep water," said the Fish; "this won't do for me." So the good-natured fellow took her and waded into the water till he was neck-deep. Then the Fish opened her mouth wide, and said—

"Now I'm going to eat you! I'll teach you to say nasty things about women."

That was a nice way of showing gratitude to the Man, wasn't it? I wonder the Man did not eat the Fish, instead of the Fish eating him. But I am afraid the Man was rather stupid. It never occurred to him that he might eat the Fish, and all he did was to scratch his head again. "That's not fair," said he; "I saved your life, and now you want to eat me. We must find some one to decide between us, and say which is right."

"All right," said the Fish; "take me up on your shoulder again, and let us find somebody."

So the Man took her up on his shoulder again, and out of the water came he. On the bank of the river grew a Crab-apple Tree, and the Man appealed to this Tree to decide their dispute. "O Tree," said he, "this Fish was lying on the sand, and I saved her life, and now she wants to eat me. Do you think that is right?"

"Of course!" said the Tree—whose temper was as crabbed as his apples—"of course! Why not? You men are always doing mischief. Here am I, an innocent Crab-apple Tree, and people come along and cut off my branches to shade themselves from the sun. I call that cool!"

The Foolish Fish

"Well," said the Man, "they want to be cool, and that's why they cut your branches off."

"Don't be a fool," squeaked the Crab-apple Tree; "you know what I mean. So as you do all this damage to us, we are right to do all we can to hurt you, and therefore this Fish has a right to eat you if she chooses."

"Come along," said the Fish, as she opened her mouth; "jump in!"

"Wait a bit," said the Man, "we must try somebody else. I feel sure there is something wrong with this judgment." The Fish did not wish to ask anybody else, but she had to agree, because they were on dry land.

So they went along until they saw an Elephant.

"O Elephant!" cried the Man, "do you see this Fish? I saved her life, and now she wants to eat me. Do you think this is right?"

"Right?" said the Elephant, "I should rather think so! Why, you men are horrid brutes, always making us carry half-a-dozen of you about on our backs, or prodding us with a spike, or something nasty. Eat you up? I only wish *I* could eat you up, and I would do it too, but nature makes me eat leaves, and you are too tough for me to digest."

So there was no comfort to be had from the Elephant.

The Fish opened her mouth wider than ever, for she was getting hungry, and said, "Now then, look sharp—in with you!"

The Man was in despair. What was he to do? "Give me one more chance," said he, "and if they all say the same, then you shall eat me."

He looked round, and not far off he saw a Jackal.

"Friend Jackal," he called out; "I say, Jackal! Stop a minute, I want to ask you something."

"All right," said the Jackal, "ask away."

"This Fish," said the Man, "was flip-flap-flopping on the sand and gasping for breath, and I saved her life; and then as soon as she got safe back into the water again, she wanted to eat me. Do you think that's right?"

"Hm," said the Jackal, "I don't quite understand. Where was the Fish?"

"Lying on the sand, you booby," said the Fish, getting angry.

"How?" asked the Jackal.

"Why," said the Fish, "what does that matter, I should like to know?"

"Can't understand," said the Jackal, looking stupidly all round and then up at the sky.

"Well," said the Fish, angrier than ever, "all you are asked to do, is to say whether or no I am to eat this Man. Can't you do that without all this bother?"

"No," said the Jackal.

"Oh dear," said the Fish, "what a stupid you must be! All right then, come along, and we'll show you." So she made the Man take her on his shoulder again, and carry her to the place where she had been lying on the sand.

"That's the place," said she.

The Jackal was not satisfied yet, but he must needs see how she lay. So the Man put her down on the sand, and the Fish began flip-flap-flopping again.

"Now then," said the Jackal to the Man, "up on the horse with you, and be off! What does the Fish matter to you? Let her die, she deserves no better."

The Foolish Fish

The Man thought this a good idea, so he got up on his horse, and off, and was more resolved than ever to keep clear of women.

But the Fish was very angry at being tricked so neatly. "You shall pay for this!" she gasped to the Jackal; "I'll come and eat you in your den."

"All right, you may try," said the Jackal, "but I fancy you will get eaten yourself." And so saying, away he scampered.

The Fish flapped and flopped, until somehow or other she managed to flap herself into the river.

After this the Fish used to sit by the roots of a fig-tree which went down into the river, with her mouth gaping, in the hope that something might fall in. The Jackal used to come down to this place to drink, and one day, as he was drinking, the Fish caught him tight by the leg.

"Oh you silly Fish," said the Jackal, "why didn't you catch my leg? You have got hold of the wrong thing," said he; "there's my leg, if you want it," pointing to the root of the fig-tree. The foolish Fish believed she had made a mistake, and let go the Jackal's leg, and took a good bite of the root. The Jackal laughed, and scampered away, crying, "Oh what a fool you are! You don't know wood from meat!"

"Never mind," said the Fish, "next time it will be my turn, and then we shall see. I'll come and eat you in your den."

Next day, when the Jackal had gone into the forest to find food, our friend the Fish jumped out of the water, and went roll, roll, rolling into the forest, until she came to the den of the Jackal; and inside the door of the Jackal's den she stood on her tail, waiting for him to come back. By-and-by back came the Jackal, sure enough; but Jackals are very cunning creatures, and he came up slinking quietly, and saw the Fish before the Fish saw him. So he called out in a loud voice, "Den, Den!"

No answer. Again he called out, "Den, Den!" This time the Fish thought that the Den was no doubt accustomed to reply when the Jackal called to it. Perhaps it was shy because she was present. Anyhow she thought she had better answer, so she called out in return, "Well, well!"

"You there?" asked the Jackal.

"Yes, I'm here all right," answered the Fish.

"Just stop a minute," said the Jackal, "and I'll be back directly."

Away he ran, and the Fish crept inside the hole, and hid. The Jackal ran about gathering dry leaves, and with the leaves he made a little pile at the mouth of his hole. Then he went to a fire which some traveller had left smouldering, and seizing a brand, he brought it and set light to the leaves at the mouth of the cave. The fire soon burned up.

"Is that nice, dear Den?" asked the Jackal.

"Very nice, thank you," said the Fish, who thought she must go on pretending.

"I'll soon make you warm," said the Jackal, and he piled on more fuel. It began to get very hot.

"That's enough now," said the Fish.

"No, no, Den dear," said the cunning Jackal, laughing to himself. More and more leaves he piled on the top of the fire. One side of the Fish got so hot that she

The Foolish Fish

turned the other. Then it got hotter and hotter, and soon the Fish expired. When the fire went out, the Jackal looked into the cave, and there was the Fish, done on both sides crisp and brown. He sat down on his haunches, and gobbled her up in a trice, and he never had a nicer dinner. That was the end of the foolish and ungrateful Fish.

The Clever Goat

A SHEPHERD was feeding his flock on the hills; and as they were going home again in the evening, one of the goats lagged behind. Now, this Goat was very old, and goats are not like men, for the older they grow the wiser they become. So this Goat, being very old indeed, was also very wise. There was a very nice clump of grass by the wayside, and the wise old Goat said to herself, "Here is the nicest grass I have seen for a long time. I'm not hungry, because I have been eating all day; but I daresay I shall soon be hungry again, so I had better eat it while I can get it." And accordingly she set to work, and very soon she had eaten it all up. Then she trotted off homeward.

As the old Goat went merrily trotting along, with her eyes on the ground, suddenly she looked up—and lo and behold! a huge Wolf sitting on a stump, and staring at her hungrily! What was she to do? To escape was impossible. She pulled her wits together, and began—

"Oh, my dear Mr. Wolf!" cried she, "how delighted

The Clever Goat

I am to see you. I have been looking for you all day, and now I've found you at last."

The Wolf was so utterly astonished that he had not a word to say at first. But after a while, he found his tongue, and thus said he—

"My good Goat, you must be out of your senses. Why, I'm accustomed to feed on goats, and here you say you are glad to see me. Who ever heard of a creature so foolish as to throw itself into the jaws of death of its own free will?"

"Ah," replied the Goat, "you don't know my Shepherd, that's quite clear. He is the kindest man in the world, and he has a special weakness for you. He was talking of you only this morning, and saying that he owes you a good turn for not gobbling up any of his sheep, though it is ever so long since he began to feed them in your forest. So he has sent me to you as a token of his esteem. I'm an old Goat, you see, and not much use to him now. 'No *ifs* and *buts*,' says he to me—'off with you, and let kind Mr. Wolf eat you for his dinner.' And so here I am. And indeed, you must not suppose I am here against my will; not at all. I could not think of disobeying our good Shepherd. And, if I did, he could sell me to the butcher, to have my throat cut, and be eaten by horrid beasts of men, who have only two legs to bless themselves with. I assure you, I much prefer being eaten by a noble four-legged gentleman like yourself."

Our Wolf was still so surprised that he could find nothing to say; and the Goat went on—

"Do not think, dear sir, that I am flattering you. Look at me and judge if a respectable old Goat of my age, and at the point of death—for I see you licking your chops—whether, I say, such a one would dare to tell lies. But, Mr. Wolf, there is one reason why I shall be sorry to die. You may not have heard of it, but it is true nevertheless that I am a famous songster, and it will be indeed a pity that a gift so rare should be lost. Will you do me one last favour, and let me sing you a song before I die? I am sure it will delight you, and you will enjoy eating me all the more afterwards."

The Wolf was very much pleased at the Goat's politeness. "Well," said he, "since you are so kind as to offer, I should like to hear what you can do in the way of music."

"All right," said our Goat, "just sit down on that hillock yonder, and I'll stay here; it won't sound so nice if I am too near you."

The Wolf trotted off to the hillock, and sat down, and waited for the Goat to begin her song.

The Goat opened her mouth, and uttered a loud "Baa-baa-baa!"

"Is that all?" asked the Wolf. He was rather disappointed, but he did not say so, for fear of being thought an ignorant lout.

"Oh no," said the Goat, "that was only tuning up, to get the pitch." Then she cried again, "Baa-baa-baa," louder than before.

Meanwhile the Shepherd was not far off, and he heard this loud Baa-baa of one of his goats. "Hullo," thought he, "what's up, I wonder?" and set off running in the direction of the sound. Just as the Wolf was getting impatient, and the Goat was opening

The Clever Goat

her mouth for another Baa-baa, up came the Shepherd,
behind the Wolf. Thwack, thwack, thwack! came his
stick on the stupid Wolf, and with a groan the Wolf
turned over and died on the spot. The Shepherd
and his wise old Goat trudged happily home
to the sheepfold, and after that the Goat
took good care to keep
with the flock.

A Crow is a Crow for Ever

THERE once was a very learned Bishop, who was very fond of bird's-nesting. One day he saw a fine large nest up in an elm-tree, and when he had climbed up he saw that it was full of young Crow-chicks. One of these chicks had such a winsome appearance, that the Bishop put him inside his hat, and took him home to the Palace.

In due time the Crow grew up, and as he heard around him continually the Bishop and his friends talking divinity, by degrees he became quite clever in divinity himself. He knew all the kings of Israel and Judah, and the cities of refuge, so that at last there was no question in a divinity paper he could not answer. Indeed, once when the examining Chaplain was ill, the Crow did his work for him.

The fame of this learned Crow spread far and wide, until at last it reached the King's ears. Now the Bishop had been expecting this all along, and ever since he found the young Crow he had been training him for a purpose. I am sorry to say he was rather a greedy man; and as he hoped to get something out of the King by

G

A Crow is a Crow for Ever

the means of this Crow, he trained him to fly towards anything that shone bright, such as gold and silver.

"When the King asks me to show off my Crow," he thought, "I will ask as a price anything the Crow may choose; and then doubtless he will fly to the King's crown, and I shall be King!"

At the first all fell out as he looked for. The King sent word to say he wanted to see the Crow. He was sitting in the garden, with his gold crown on, and all his courtiers around him; and then asked to hear him say all the kings of Israel and Judah.

"With pleasure, sire," said the Bishop; "if your Majesty will deign to grant him what he chooses for a reward. He has been well taught, and will not work for nothing."

"By all means," said the King; "let him choose his reward, and I will give it."

Then the Bishop took his Crow out of his hat, and the Crow said all the kings of Israel and Judah quite right, forwards and backwards, without a single mistake. The King was delighted: he could not have done as much.

"And now, sire," said the Bishop, "I will let him go, and tell him to choose his own prize."

So the Bishop let the Crow loose. The Crow was flying straight for the King's crown, when all on a sudden what should he spy but a dead cat! He turned off on the instant, and down he swooped on the dead cat. You know Crows eat dead things and offal; and this Crow liked a dead cat for dinner better than a gold crown.

The King laughed, the courtiers roared with merriment.

"Bishop," said the King, when he had done laughing, "your Crow is easily pleased, it seems! Well, he has chosen his reward, and by my royal beard, he shall have it. Ha, ha, ha!"

But the Bishop felt very rueful indeed. All his pains and trouble lost, and nothing to show for it! He shook his head and went away, singing to himself a little chant he made up on the spot, all out of his own head—

> "I kept my Crow in a lovely cage,
> And taught him wisdom's holy page;
> But still 'tis true, whate'er he may know,
> A dirty Crow is a dirty Crow."

The Grateful Goat

ONCE upon a time a Butcher bought a Goat; but as he was going to kill the Goat, and make him into meat for the table, the Goat opened his mouth, and said—

"If you kill me, Butcher, you will be a few shillings the richer; but if you spare my life, I will repay you for your kindness."

This Butcher had killed many goats in his day, but he never before heard one of them talk. Goats can talk to each other, as you must have heard; but most of them do not learn English. So the Butcher thought there must be something special about this Goat, and did not kill him.

The Goat felt very grateful that his life had been spared for a few more happy summers; and when he found himself free, the first thing he did was to go into the forest to see if he could find some means of repaying the Butcher's kind deed.

As he trotted along under the trees, stopping now and then to crop some tender shoot that came within reach, he met a Jackal.

"I am glad to see you, Goatee," said the Jackal; "and now I'm going to eat you."

"Don't be such a fool," said the Goat. "Can't you see I am nothing but skin and bones? Wait till I get fat. That's why I am here, just to get fat; and when I'm nice and fat, you may eat me and welcome."

The Goat was very skinny, in truth, and he pulled in his breath to make himself look more skinny. So the Jackal said—

"All right, look sharp, and be sure you look out for me on your way back."

"I shan't forget, Jackal," said the Goat. "Ta ta!"

By-and-by he fell in with a Wolf.

"Ha!" said the Wolf, smacking his lips; "here's what I want. Get ready, my Goat, for I am going to eat you."

"Oh, surely not," said the Goat; "a skinny old thing like me!" He drew in his breath again, and looked very skinny indeed. "I have come here to fatten myself, and when I'm fat, you shall eat me if you like."

"Well," said the Wolf, "you don't look like a prize Goat, I grant you. Go along then, but look out for me when you come back."

"Oh, I shall look out for you!" said the Goat, and away he trotted.

By-and-by he came to a church. He went into the church, and there he saw last Sunday's collection plate, full of gold coins. In that country, any one would have been ashamed to put coppers into the plate, not because they were rich, for they were not, but because they were generous. Now, Goats are not taught that they must not steal, but they think they have a right to whatever they can get hold of; so this Goat opened his mouth,

The Grateful Goat

and licked up all the sovereigns, and hid them under his tongue.

The Goat next went to a flower-shop, and asked the man who sold the flowers to make some wreaths, and cover him up with them, horns and all. So the man covered him up with flowers, till he looked like a large rose-bush. Then the Goat popped out a sovereign from his mouth, to pay the man, and very glad the man was to get so much for his roses.

Then the Goat set out on his homeward way. He looked out for the Wolf, as he had promised to do; and when the Wolf saw him coming along, he thought he was a rose-bush. The Wolf was not at all surprised to see a rose-bush walking along the road, for many were the strange things he had seen in his life; and if you come to think of it, this was no stranger than a Goat that could talk English.

"Good afternoon, Rose-bush," said the Wolf; "have you seen a Goat passing this way?"

"Oh yes," said the Goat, "I saw him a few minutes ago back there along the road."

"Many thanks, Rose-bush," said the Wolf; "I am much obliged to you," and away he ran in the direction in which the Goat had come.

By-and-by he came to the Jackal.

"Hullo, Rose-bush!" said the Jackal. "Have you seen a Goat anywhere as you came along?"

"Oh yes," replied the Goat, out of the roses; "I saw him just now, and he was talking to a big Wolf."

"Good heavens!" said the Jackal, "I must look sharp, if I want some Goat to-day," and off he galloped, in a great hurry.

In the evening he got to the Butcher's house.

"Hullo!" said the Butcher, "what have we here?" He knew that rose-bushes could not walk, but he could not make out what it was at all.

"Baa! baa!" said the Goat; "it's your grateful old Goat, come back to pay you for your kindness." And with these words, he spouted out all the sovereigns he found in the church, except the one he paid to the flower-man.

The Butcher was delighted to see so many sovereigns: he asked no questions, because he thought it wiser. He took the sovereigns, and found they were enough to keep him all his life, without killing any more goats. So he lived in peace, and the Goat spent his remaining years browsing comfortably in the Butcher's paddock.

The Cunning Jackal

Or, The Biter Bit

A JACKAL lived on one side of a deep river, and on the other side were fields upon fields of ripe melons. The Jackal was always hungry, and he had eaten everything within reach; so he used to sit on the river bank and bemoan his luck. "All those ripe melons," said he, "and nobody to eat them but men. It is really a shame. I don't know what Providence is doing, to treat me so scurvily."

Perhaps Providence knew what it was about, and the Jackal, as you shall hear, deserved no better than he got.

As he sat one day by the river, moaning and groaning, a big Tortoise popped up his funny head out of the water. There was a big tear in each of the Tortoise's round eyes.

The Jackal stopped moaning and groaning when he saw the Tortoise. "What's the matter, Shelly?" said he. "Aren't you well?"

"Quite well, thank you," said the Tortoise, and the tears slowly rolled down his nose. He was going to call the Jackal Snarly, which was the nickname the Jackal went by; but he thought better of it, because it would have been rather rude. All the same, he did not like being called Shelly in that offhand way.

"Wife and brats all right?" asked the Jackal. "No measles or mumps?"

This was also very rude of the Jackal, because a Tortoise is sensitive about mumps. If he gets mumps when his head is inside his shell, he can't put it out; and if his head is outside, that is still worse, for it swells up so that he can't get it in again.

"No, thank you, my wife is all right," said the Tortoise, who was rather confused; "at least, she would be all right if I had one, but that's just it—I can't get a wife! Nobody will look at me! and that is my trouble," and two more big tears trickled down his nose.

At this moment an idea came into the Jackal's crafty head. "What a pity you didn't tell me before," said he; "I could easily have found you a wife last week, but now she has gone to live on the other side of the river."

"Do you really mean it?" said the Tortoise.

"Honour bright," answered the Jackal; "do I look like a person who would tell a lie?" He certainly did, only the Tortoise was too simple to see it.

The Tortoise rubbed away his tears on a stump, for he had no handkerchief, and brightened up considerably.

"I can carry you across, friend," said he, "if you will jump on my back."

The Jackal wanted nothing better, so down he jumped on the back of the Tortoise, and the Tortoise swam across. When they got across, the Tortoise was quite

The Cunning Jackal

tired, because the Jackal was very heavy for a Tortoise to carry.

A fine time the Jackal had on the further side of the river. He ran about among the fields, and ate melons till he was nearly bursting. Every day the Tortoise came to the bank, asking whether the match was yet arranged, and every day the Jackal told him that all was going well. "You have no notion how pleased they are," said the Jackal. "Just see how fat I am getting. They feed me like a fighting-cock, all because of you." It was indeed because of the Tortoise that the Jackal was so well fed, but not as he meant it.

By-and-by the season of melons came to an end, and all that the Jackal had left were cut and sold in the market. Melons were dear that season, because the Jackal had eaten so many of them before they could be cut. Then the Jackal stole a white dress and a veil, and hung them on the stump of a tree which stood near the river side; and next day, when the Tortoise popped his funny head out of the water, said the Jackal—

"There's your wife at last, old Shelly! There she stands, dumb as a stone. Not a word will she have to say to you till I am out of the way, because she is too modest. Come, hurry up, Shell-fish, and take me across."

The Tortoise was angry at being called a shell-fish, because tortoises are not fish at all, and they feel insulted if you call them so. However, he was so glad to get a wife at last, that he said nothing, only presented his back for the Jackal to jump on. Flop! came the Jackal, so heavy by this time that it was all the Tortoise could do to get him across safely. If he was tired before, he was nearly dead now. But he swam across at last; and the Jackal ran off into the forest, chuckling at the simplicity of the poor Tortoise.

Back went our Tortoise across the river, and climbed up on the bank.

"Wife!" he called out, in a tender voice.

No answer.

Again he called "Wife!" but still no answer.

He could not make it out a bit. He crawled up to the stump which the Jackal had decked out in wedding finery, and put out his flapper to touch his wife's hand: lo and behold, it was only an old tree-stump.

The rage of the Tortoise knew no bounds, and he determined to have his revenge.

Next day the Jackal came down to drink at the river. The Tortoise was watching for him under water; and while the Jackal was drinking, the Tortoise nipped his teeth into the Jackal's leg.

How the Jackal did howl, to be sure! He was a great coward, and even used to cry when his teeth were pulled out by the dentist. So now he howled at the top of his voice, "Let me go! Let me go!"

But the Tortoise held on like grim death. He was too weak to pull the Jackal under, but he was too heavy for the Jackal to pull out; so there he bides his time. By-and-by the tide began to rise. The tide rose to the Jackal's middle, it rose to his head; and his last howls came up from underneath the water in big bubbles, which showed that the crafty Jackal would play his mean tricks never more.

The Farmer's Ass

THERE was once a Farmer, who had an Ass. It was the habit of this Ass to lift up his voice and bray, whenever he heard the church bells a-ringing. Now in the country where this Farmer lived, they used to believe that a man's soul passes when he dies into an animal, or something else. So this Farmer thought that any Ass that was fond of church bells, must have been a great saint in some former life. Accordingly, he named his Ass St. Anthony.

All his life long, this Ass served the Farmer faithfully, and earned him a great deal of money. At last the Ass died of old age.

The Farmer was very sad and sorry when his Ass died. "My Ass served me faithfully," said he, "and it's only fair he should have a good funeral." So he sent for the undertaker, and told him to make a big coffin, and put it on a hearse, and buried the Ass with great splendour. Then he shaved off every scrap of hair from his head, as the custom was in those parts when anybody died, and gave a funeral feast to all his relations, and dressed himself in black.

Next time he went to the Grocer's to buy sugar, the Grocer noticed his head shaved bare, and the black clothes, so he knew some one must be dead, a relation or a great friend.

"I am sorry to see you have lost some one," said he; "who is it?"

"St. Anthony is dead," said the Farmer.

"Dear me," said the Grocer, "and I never heard of it. How very sad!" Thought he to himself, "I had best have my head shaved too, or else people will call me hard-hearted."

So when the Farmer had bought his sugar, and was gone, the Grocer went to the Barber and had his head shaved. Then he put on a black coat and necktie.

By-and-by a Soldier came to have a chat with his friend the Grocer.

"Ods bobs!" said he, "what's the matter, man?"

"St. Anthony is dead," said the Grocer solemnly, and wiped away a tear.

"You don't say so," said the Soldier. Off he went straight to the Barber, and made him shave his head; then he bought a piece of crape to tie round his left arm.

He told the news to all the men of his regiment, and they all felt so much sympathy with this soldier that they shaved their heads too.

Next day on parade, there was the whole regiment shaved to a man.

"What's the meaning of this?" asked the General.

The Sergeant saluted, and told him that St. Anthony was dead.

"Is he? By Jove," said the General, "then I dismiss this parade," and off he galloped on his war-horse to

The Farmer's Ass

the nearest Barber, who shaved his head like the men's. On the way back, he saw the Prime Minister going to Court. "May I ask," said the Prime Minister suavely, "to what untoward circumstance is due the erasure of your capillary covering?"

"St. Anthony is dead," answered the General.

"Dear, dear," said the Prime Minister, "you don't say so. He was doubtless an ornament to the party, and it is meet that I should testify my respect." Then the Prime Minister too went off to get his head shaved, and appeared before the King without a single hair.

"What's the matter?" asked the King; "anybody dead, hey, hey, hey?"

"If it please your Majesty," said the Prime Minister, "St. Anthony is dead."

"What a loss for our kingdom," said the King; "what a loss! what a loss! Excuse me a moment," and away he went to get his head shaved.

When the Queen saw him, she wanted to know why his head was shaved.

"St. Anthony is dead," answered the King.

"And who is St. Anthony?" asked the Queen.

"I don't know who he is," said the King, "a friend of the Prime Minister's."

So the Prime Minister was asked who St. Anthony was; and replied that he did not himself know him, but the General spoke of him in the highest terms. The General said that St. Anthony was not a personal friend, but he was well known in the regiment. After inquiry amongst the men, it was found that only one of them could tell anything about St. Anthony, and all he knew was that his friend the Grocer shaved his head in memory of him. The Grocer referred them to the Farmer, and the Farmer was out in the fields.

Then the King sent a messenger on horseback to find the Farmer and bring him to court. The Farmer was brought into court, and when he saw the King and the Prime Minister and General all in mourning, he was very much surprised. The King said to him, "Farmer, who is St. Anthony?"

"If it please your Majesty, he was my Ass."

The King, and the Prime Minister, and the General felt very foolish to have gone into mourning for an Ass. They put off their black clothes, but it was not so easy to get their hair back again; and so for a month or two the King, and the Prime Minister, and the General, and all the regiment of Body Guards, went about in wigs.

The Parrot Judge

THERE was once a Fowler who caught a young Parrot. He kept the Parrot in his house, hoping that it would pick up something to say, but the Parrot learnt nothing at all. Then he set to work at teaching it; but after six months the Parrot had only learnt to say two things: one was "Of course," and the other was "Certainly."

Seeing that his trouble was wasted, the Fowler took him to market in a gilt cage, in order to catch the eye of customers. He cried in a loud voice, "Who'll buy! who'll buy! here's a Parrot which can say anything in the world! Here's a clever Parrot who knows what he is talking about! If you want a question answered here's the Parrot to answer you, no matter what it may be! Who'll buy, who'll buy?" Everybody crowded round to see the wonderful Parrot.

The King happened to be passing by, and heard all this to-do about a Parrot. Said he to the Fowler—

"Is it really true about your Parrot?"

"Ask him, sire," said the Fowler.

"Parrot," said the King, "do you know English?"

"Of course," said the Parrot, in a tone of scorn, turning up his beak; as who should say, "What a question to ask *me*."

"Can you decide knotty points of law?" the King went on.

"Certainly," said the Parrot, with great confidence.

"This is the bird for me," said the King, and asked his price. The price was a thousand pounds. The King paid a thousand pounds to the Fowler, and departed.

A big price, you will say, for a Parrot. So it was; but the King had a reason for paying it. The Judge of the City had just died, and the King could not find another. Hundreds of men offered to do the work. Some wanted too much money, more than the King could pay; some were reasonable, but knew no law; and the cheaper ones who professed to know everything were all Germans, whom the King would not have at any price. When he heard of this wise Parrot, thought he, "Here's my Judge; he will want no wages but sugar and chickweed, and he will take no bribes."

So the Parrot was made Judge, and sat on a big throne, with a white wig and a red robe lined with ermine.

Next day, the Parrot was in Court, and a case came up for judgment. It was a murder case, and when the evidence had been heard, the pleader on the murderer's side finished up his speech by saying, "And now, my Lord, you must admit that my client is innocent."

Said the Parrot, "Of course."

The Parrot Judge

Everybody thought this rather odd, because the other side had not yet been heard; and, besides, the man was caught in the act. However, they held their tongues and waited.

Then the prosecutor got up, and made a long speech, at the end of which he said, "It is no longer possible to doubt that the prisoner at the bar is guilty. Two witnesses saw him do the deed, and half-a-dozen caught him just as he was pulling the knife out of the body. I therefore call upon you, my Lord, to pass sentence of death."

Said the Parrot, "Certainly."

At this the King pricked up his ears. The man could not be innocent of course, and yet certainly guilty, at the same time. So he turned to the Judge and said—

"If you go against evidence so clear, Judge, I shall begin to suspect that you killed the man yourself."

Said the Parrot, "Certainly."

You may imagine the hubbub that arose in Court when the Judge said this! Everybody saw that the King had made a mistake in his Judge, and even the King himself began to suspect that something was wrong. So he said, rather angrily, to the Parrot—

"Then it is your head ought to be chopped off."

Said the Parrot, "Of course."

"Chop off his head, then," cried the King; and they took away the Parrot and chopped off his head without delay; and all the while he was being dragged along, he called out,
"Certainly," "Certainly,"
"Certainly."

The Frog and the Snake

A FROG and a Snake had a quarrel as to which could give the more deadly bite. They agreed to try it on the next opportunity.

A Man came to bathe in the pond where these two creatures lived. The Snake bit him under the water, while the Frog floated on the top. "Something has bitten me!" the Man called out to his friends.

"What is it?" they asked.

Then he saw the Frog swimming on the top of the water. "Oh, it's only a Frog," said he. Then he went away, and no harm came of it.

The next time that Man came to bathe in the pond, the Frog bit him under the water, while the Snake swam on the top.

"Oh dear!" said the Man, "a Snake has bitten me!" The Man died.

"Now," said the Frog, "you will admit that my bite is more poisonous than yours."

"I deny it altogether," said the Snake.

So they agreed to refer their dispute to the King of the Snakes. The Snake King listened to their arguments, and decided in favour of the Snake, and said the Man had died of fright.

"Of course," grumbled the Frog, "the Snake King sides with the Snake."

So both of them bit the Frog, and he died, and that was the end of him.

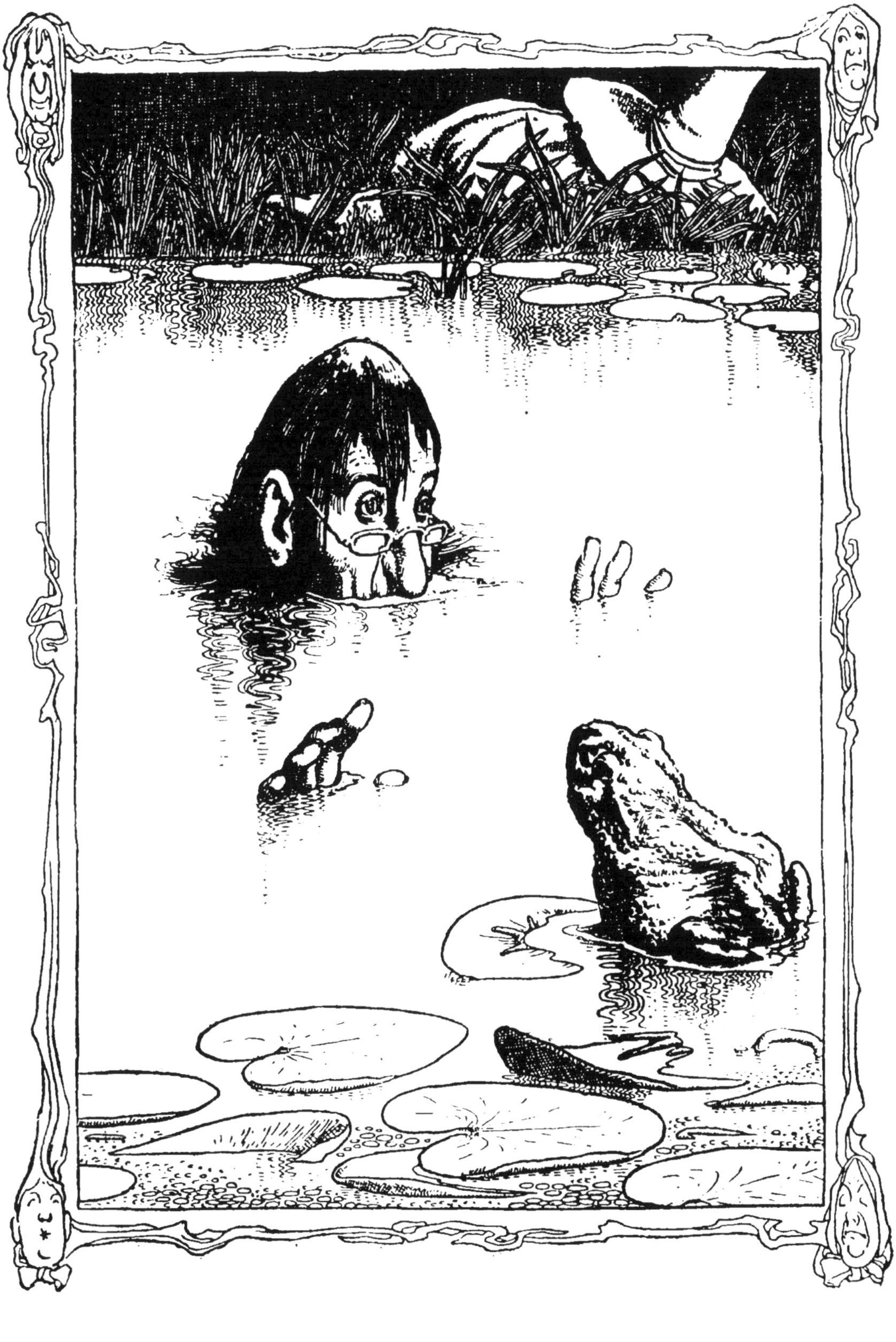

Little Miss Mouse and her Friends

THERE was once a little Lady-Mouse that lived in a field. She was all alone in the world, a little old maid, and she very much wanted a friend. But every creature turned up his nose at the poor little Mouse, and not a friend could she get; until at last a Clod of earth took pity upon her. Then the Mouse and the Clod became firm friends, and went about everywhere together. The Mouse walked upon her four legs, and the Clod rolled along like a cricket ball.

One day the Mouse wanted a bathe; and nothing would serve, but the Clod must go bathe along with her. In vain the Clod protested that she did not like water; that she had never washed in her life; that she could not swim: Miss Mousie would take no denial, and said severely, that if the Clod had never washed before, it was high time to begin. So at length the Clod was persuaded, and into the river they went. Mousie went in first, and the Clod rolled in afterwards; but no sooner had the poor Clod rolled into the river, than what was

Miss Mousie's horror to see her melt away in the water, and disappear.

Mousie was now friendless again, and loudly complained to the River that he had stolen away her favourite Clod.

"I am very sorry," the River said; "I really couldn't help melting a thing so soft. I can't give you back your Clod, but I will give you a Fish instead."

This comforted Mousie, and she took her Fish and went home. Then she put the Fish on the top of a post, to dry. Down swooped a big Kite, and flew away with the Fish.

"O my poor Fish," wailed Miss Mousie, "to be taken away before we had a word together." Then she went to the Post, and demanded her Fish back again. "I gave him to you," said Mousie, "and you are responsible for him."

Said the Post, "I am very sorry that I cannot give you back your Fish, but I will give you some Wood."

Mousie was grateful for this kindness on the part of the Post. So she took a piece of Wood in exchange for the Fish.

Mousie and the Wood went off to buy some sweets at the Confectioner's. While Mousie was eating the sweets, the Confectioner's wife burnt the Wood in the fire.

Mousie finished the sweets, and when she turned round to look for her Wood, lo and behold it was gone. With tears in her eyes she begged the Confectioner's wife to give her back the Wood, but the Confectioner's wife said—

"I am very sorry I cannot give you back the Wood,

Little Miss Mouse

because it is burnt; but I will give you some Cakes instead."

This made Miss Mousie happy again, and she took the Cakes. Then she paid a visit to the Shepherd's pen; and while she was talking to the Shepherd, a Goat ate up her cakes.

"Give me back my Cakes, Mr. Shepherd," said Mousie, not seeing the Cakes anywhere.

"I'm very sorry I can't do that," answered the Shepherd, "because I am afraid one of my goats has eaten them; but if you like, you may have a Kid instead."

This was better and better. Mousie was charmed with her Kid and led it off to the music-shop, where she had to pay a bill. While the man was writing a receipt to the bill, his wife killed the Kid, and began to roast it for dinner. Mousie looked round, and wanted to know where her Kid was?

"I rather think," said the Music-man, "that the nice odour of roast meat which tickles your nostrils, comes from that Kid. I'm sorry I can't give you the Kid back, but you may have the best drum in my shop."

Mousie did not like the Drum so well as her Kid; but needs must, and she picked out a drum, and went away with it on her shoulder. By-and-by she came to a place where women were beating rice, to get the grains away from the husk. She hung up her Drum on a peg, while she watched the women husking the rice. Bang! flap! a woman drove her pestle right through the Drum.

Poor Mousie. It seemed as if her misfortunes would never end. When she asked the woman for her Drum again, there it was, burst. The tears ran down her cheeks.

"We are very sorry," the women all said, "that we cannot give you back your Drum; but you can have a Girl instead, if you like."

This brought smiles to Miss Mousie's sad face, and she dried her tears. The women gave her a nice Girl, and Mousie took the Girl home. They set up house together, and planted a crop of corn. The corn ripened, and they went out to cut it. Miss Mouse was a wee mousie, and was quite hidden among the stalks of the corn. While the Girl was cutting the corn with a sickle, she did not see poor little Mousie, so she cut her in two, and that was the end of her.

The Jackal that Lost his Tail

THERE was once a Farmer, who used to go out every morning to work in his field, and his wife used to bring him dinner at noon. One day, as the Farmer's wife was carrying out the dinner to the field, she met a Jackal, who said—

"Where are you going?"

Said she, "To my husband, and this is his dinner."

Said the Jackal, "Give me some, or I will bite you."

So the woman had to give the Jackal some of this food. And when her husband saw it, he said—

"What a small dinner you have brought me to-day!"

"A Jackal met me," replied his wife, "and threatened to bite me if I gave him none."

"All right," said the Farmer, "to-morrow I'll settle with that Jackal."

On the morrow, the Farmer's wife went after the plough, and the Farmer dressed up in her clothes and carried out the dinner. Again the Jackal appeared.

"Give me some of that," said he, "or I'll bite you."

"Yes, yes, good Mr. Jackal," said the man, "you shall have some, only don't bite me."

The Jackal that Lost his Tail

Then he set down the plate and the Jackal began to eat.

"Just scratch my back, you, woman," said the Jackal, "while I am eating my dinner."

"Yes, sir; yes, sir," said the man. He began gently to tickle and scratch the back of the Jackal, and in the middle, suddenly out with his knife, and slish! cut off the Jackal's tail.

The Jackal jumped up and capered about. "Yow-ow-ow!" he went, "what has come to my tail? Oh dear! how shall I swish away the flies? Oh dear, how it hurts! Yow-ow-ow!" Away he scuttled, as fast as his legs could carry him.

When he got home, all the Jackals came round him, and asked what had become of his tail. The Jackal was ashamed to have lost his tail, which was a particularly long and fine tail; but he pretended to like it.

"Poor fellow!" said the Jackals, "where is your tail?"

"I had it cut off," said the Jackal, "and good riddance. It was always in my way. Why, I never could sit down in comfort, and now look here!" He sat down on the place where his tail used to be, and looked proudly round. "Now, you try!" said he.

The Jackal that Lost his Tail

They all tried, and found that their tails got underneath them when they sat, and it hurt their tails rather.

"We never thought of that before," said they; "we must get rid of these things. Who cut off yours?"

"A kind Farmer's wife," said the first Jackal. Then he told them where the Farmer's wife lived.

That evening, a knock came at the Farmer's door, as the Farmer and his wife were sitting at tea.

"Come in!" said the Farmer.

The door opened, and in trooped a number of Jackals. "Please, Mr. Farmer," said they, "we want you kindly to cut off our tails."

"Willingly," said the Farmer; whipt out his knife, and in a jiffy slish! slish! slish! off came the Jackals' tails.

"Yow-ow-ow!" went the Jackals, capering about, "we didn't think it would hurt!" Away they went, and all the woods echoed that night with yowling and howling.

When they all got home, they found the first Jackal waiting for them. He laughed in their faces. "Now we're all alike," said he, "all in the same boat."

"Are we?" said the other Jackals, and set on him and tore him to pieces.

"Now we must have our revenge on the Farmer," said the Jackals when they had eaten up their friend. So next morning they scampered off to the Farmer's house.

The Farmer was out, and his wife was gathering fuel.

"Good morning, Mrs. Farmer," said the Jackals; "we have come to eat the Farmer for cutting our tails off."

"Ah, poor fellow," said the Farmer's wife, "he is dead. When he saw how it hurt you to have your tails cut off, he just lay down on the bed, and died of grief."

"That's unlucky," said the Jackals.

"But we are preparing the funeral feast," she went on, "you see I am now getting fuel for it. Will you give us the pleasure of your company to dinner?"

"Gladly," said the Jackals; "we should like to see the last of the poor fellow;" then they ran away.

At dinner-time, they all came back, and found chairs put for them, and plates round the table, with the woman at one end.

"You can sit like Christians now," said the Farmer's wife, "so I have set you a chair apiece."

"Thanks," said the Jackals; "that is thoughtful."

"But I know," the Farmer's wife went on, "what quarrelsome creatures you are over your meat. Don't you think I had better tie you to your chairs, and then each will have to keep to his own plateful?"

"A good plan," the Jackals said, wagging their heads. They had now no tails to wag, and they had to wag something. So the Farmer's wife tied them tight to their chairs.

"But how shall we eat?" said the Jackals, who could not stir a paw.

"Oh, no fear for that, I'll feed you."

Then she brought out a steaming mess, and put it in the middle of the table. All the Jackals sniffed at the steam, and all their eyes were fixed greedily upon the meat. They began to struggle.

"Softly, softly, good Jackals!" said the Farmer's wife.

The Jackal that Lost his Tail

But what a surprise awaited the Jackals! They were so intent upon watching the Farmer's wife and the meat, that none of them heard the door open, and none of them saw the Farmer himself creep softly in, with a great club in his hand. The first news they had of it was crack! crack! crack!

All but three of the Jackals looked round, and they saw these three of their comrades with their heads smashed in, lolling back in the chairs. The Farmer held the club poised in the air; down it came crack! on the head of the fourth Jackal. Then all the others began yowling and struggling to get free; but in vain, the cords held them fast, they could not stir; and in five minutes all the Jackals lay dead on the floor.

After that the Farmer ploughed in peace, and no one molested the Farmer's wife when she brought his dinner.

The Wily Tortoise

A FOWLER was bird-catching in the jungle, and snared a wild goose. As he was carrying home his goose, he sat down by a pond. In this pond lived a Tortoise, and the Tortoise put up his nose out of the pond to sniff the air. He saw the Fowler and the Goose, and being a very innocent Tortoise, he feared no harm, but began to waddle towards them.

"Take care, friend!" said the Goose. "This Fowler has caught me, and he will catch you!"

The Tortoise waddled into the water again. "Many thanks, friend," said he. "One good turn deserves another." So saying, he dived down into the pond, and brought up a ruby.

"Here, Mr. Fowler," said he, "take this ruby, and let my friend the Goose go."

The Fowler took the ruby, but he was very greedy, so he said—

"If you will bring me a pair to this, I will let the Goose go."

The Tortoise dived down, and brought up another ruby. Then the Fowler let go the Goose, and said to the Tortoise, "Now hand over that ruby."

The Wily Tortoise

The Tortoise said, "Forgive me, I have made a mistake, and brought up the wrong ruby. Let me see the first, and if it does not match, I will try again."

The Fowler gave back the first ruby. "As I thought," said the Tortoise. Down he dived into the pond.

The Fowler waited a good long time, but nothing was seen of the Tortoise. As you have guessed, when the Tortoise found himself safe at the bottom of the pond, he stayed there. The Fowler tore his hair, and went home, wishing he had not been so greedy.

The King of the Mice

FAR away in the forest was the Kingdom of Mouseland. There was a great city, where every Mouse had his little house, with doors and windows, tables and chairs, books for the grown-up Mice, and toys for the children; there were little shops, where the Mice bought clothes and food, and everything they wanted; there was a little church where they went on Sunday, and a reverend little Mouse in a little lawn surplice to preach to them; there was a little palace, and in this palace lived the little Mouse King.

Now it happened that a caravan passed through the Kingdom of the Mice. Not that the men of the caravan knew what a wonderful kingdom they were in. They thought it was just like any other part of the forest, and if they did happen to pass a Mouse fortress, or farmyard, they thought them nothing but heaps of earth. Just so if you were to fly up in a balloon, and look down on your own house from the air, it would seem like a little doll's-house, not fit for a child to live in. This caravan, as I have said, was passing through Mouseland, and encamped in part of it once to spend the night. One

The King of the Mice

of the Camels was very sick, and as the owner of the Camel thought it was sure to die, he left it behind when the caravan went away.

But the Camel did not die; he very soon got as well as ever he was. And when he got well he also got hungry; so he strode all over Mouseland, eating up the crops of the Mice, and treading their houses down, until at last he came to the Mouse King's park. He ate a great many trees in the Mouse King's park, and the Keeper went in a hurry and flurry to tell the King.

"O King," said he, "a mountain several miles high has walked into your park, and is eating everything up."

"We must make an example of this mountain," said the King, "or the whole earth may be moving next. Sandy," said he to his Prime Minister, who was a Fox, "go and fetch that mountain to me."

So Sandy the Prime Minister went to seek the mountain that was eating the King's park. Next morning, back he came, leading the Camel by his nose-string.

When the Camel saw how little the King of the Mice seemed to be, he began to grunt and gurgle, and sniffed with his funny mouth. You know a Camel has a mouth which looks as though it had two slits in it, of the shape of a cross; and when he wants to show his contempt for anything he pokes out his mouth like a four-leaved clover, and makes you feel very small. "Hullo," said the Camel, "is this your King? I thought it was the Lion who sent for me. I would never have come for a speck like this." Then he turned round, and walked out of court, and began to eat everything he came across.

The King was very angry, but what could he do? He had to swallow the insult, and make the best of it.

However, he determined to watch his chance of revenge; and soon he got it. For after a few days, the Camel's nose-string became entangled in a creeper, and he could not get away, do what he would. Then Sandy the Fox came by, and saw him in this plight. Imagine his joy to see his enemy at his mercy! Off he ran, and soon brought the King to that place. Then the King said—

"O Camel, you despised my words, and see the result. Your sin has found you out."

"O mighty King," said the Camel, quite humble now, "indeed I confess my fault, and I pray you to forgive me. If you will only save me, I will be your faithful servant."

The Mouse King was not of a spiteful nature, and as soon as he heard the Camel ask forgiveness his heart grew soft. He climbed up the creeper, and gnawed through the Camel's nose-string, and set the Camel free.

The Camel, I am glad to say, kept his word; and he became a servant of the Mouse King. He was so big and strong that he could carry loads which would have needed thousands of Mice to carry; and by his help the King made very strong walls and forts around his city, so that he had no fear of enemies. When there was nothing else to do, the Camel even blacked the Mouse King's boots, rather than be idle.

So things went on for a long time. But one day some Woodcutters came into the forest. These men lived all together in a village of their own, and they used to build houses of wood. When anybody wanted a house, he told the Woodcutters, and they used to leave their village and go into the woods. Then they cut down the trees, and sawed them into planks, and shaped

The King of the Mice

them into the parts of a house. When the house was finished, they put numbers on all the parts, and took it to pieces again, and put it on a raft; and the raft floated down the great river to the place where the house had been ordered. Then they put up the house in a very short time, because you see it was all ready made, and only had to be put together.

These Woodcutters, then, came and settled for a while near the borders of Mouseland; and in the course of their wanderings they found the stray Camel. They promptly seized him, and carried him off.

When Sandy told the King what had happened, the Mouse King was very angry indeed. He sent a detachment of his bodyguard, armed cap-à-pie, to fetch the Woodcutters into his presence. The bodyguard captured two of them, and led them back bound. Then the King demanded his Camel.

"Pooh, silly little Mouse," said the Woodcutters. "If you want it, you must fetch it."

"I will," said the King of the Mice. "Tell your chief, whoever he is, that I hereby declare war upon him."

The Woodcutters laughed, and went away.

Then the Mouse King gathered together all his subjects, millions and millions of sturdy Mice; and they set out for the village of the Woodcutters. The Woodcutters had by this time finished their job, and they had been paid a good round sum of money for it; and the money was carefully put away, with all the other money they had, in a treasury.

Now the Mice were not able to meet big Woodcutters in the field, but they had their own tactics. Night and day they burrowed under the earth. First they made for the treasury; and though the treasury had stone walls, they got up easily through the floor, where no danger was expected, and one by one they carried off every coin from the treasury, until it was as bare as the palm of your hand. Then they got underneath all the houses of the village; and thousands and millions of Mice were busy all day and all night in carrying out little baskets of earth from beneath the foundations. Thus it happened, that very soon the Woodcutters' village was standing on a thin shell of earth, and underneath it was a great hole.

Now was the time to strike the blow. The layer of earth was so thin, that the least shock would destroy it. So the Mouse King wrote a letter to the Woodcutter Chief, asking once more for his Camel, and in the letter he hid a little packet of snuff. He put the letter in the post, and waited.

Next day, as the Woodcutter Chief was sitting in his house, the postman came to the door—Rat-tat. The footman brought in a letter, and the Woodcutter Chief opened it. He read it through, and laughed. Then he waved it in the air, and said, "Let them come." As he waved the letter in the air, all the snuff fell out of it upon his nose. The Woodcutter gave a terrific sneeze, Tishoo! Tishoo! The thin shell of earth could not stand the shock; it trembled, and crumbled, and fell in, and all the Woodcutters fell in too, and all their village, and nothing was left of them but a big hole.

Then the Mouse King and his army went back to Mouseland; and though they never got the old Camel back (for he was swallowed up along with the Woodcutters), yet no one ever molested Mouseland again.

The Valiant Blackbird

A BLACKBIRD and his mate lived together on a tree. The Blackbird used to sing very sweetly, and one day the King heard him in passing by, and sent a Fowler to catch him. But the Fowler made a mistake; he did not catch Mr. Blackbird, who sang so sweetly, but Mrs. Blackbird, who could hardly sing at all. However, he did not know the difference, to look at her, nor did the King when he got the bird; but a cage was made for Mrs. Blackbird, and there she was kept imprisoned.

When Mr. Blackbird heard that his dear spouse was stolen, he was very angry indeed. He determined to get her back, by hook or by crook. So he got a long sharp thorn, and tied it at his waist by a thread; and on his head he put the half of a walnut-shell for a helmet, and the skin of a dead frog served for body-armour. Then he made a little kettle-drum out of the other half of the walnut-shell; and he beat his drum, and proclaimed war upon the King.

As he walked along the road, beating his drum, he met a Cat.

"Whither away, Mr. Blackbird?" said the Cat.

"To fight against the King," said Mr. Blackbird.

"All right," said the Cat, "I'll come with you: he drowned my kitten."

"Jump into my ear, then," says Mr. Blackbird. The Cat jumped into the Blackbird's ear, and curled up, and went to sleep: and the Blackbird marched along, beating his drum.

Some way further on, he met some Ants.

"Whither away, Mr. Blackbird?" said the Ants.

"To fight against the King," said Mr. Blackbird.

"All right," said the Ants, "we'll come too; he poured hot water down our hole."

"Jump into my ear," said Mr. Blackbird. In they jumped, and away went Blackbird, beating upon his drum.

Next he met a Rope and a Club. They asked him, whither away? and when they heard that he was going to fight against the King, they jumped into his ear also, and away he went.

Not far from the King's palace, Blackbird had to cross over a River.

"Whither away, friend Blackbird?" asked the River.

Quoth the Blackbird, "To fight against the King."

"Then I'll come with you," said the River.

"Jump into my ear," says the Blackbird.

Blackbird's ears were pretty full by this time, but he found room somewhere for the River, and away he went.

The Valiant Blackbird

Blackbird marched along until he came to the palace of the King. He knocked at the door, thump, thump.

"Who's there?" said the Porter.

"General Blackbird, come to make war upon the King, and get back his wife."

The Porter laughed so at the sight of General Blackbird, with his thorn, and his frogskin, and his drum, that he nearly fell off his chair. Then he escorted Blackbird into the King's presence.

"What do you want?" said the King.

"I want my wife," said the Blackbird, beating upon his drum, rub-a-dub-dub, rub-a-dub-dub.

"You shan't have her," said the King.

"Then," said the Blackbird, "you must take the consequences." Rub-a-dub-dub went the drum.

"Seize this insolent bird," said the King, "and shut him up in the henhouse. I don't think there will be much left of him in the morning."

The servants shut up Blackbird in the henhouse. When all the world was asleep, Blackbird said—

> "Come out, Pussy, from my ear,
> There are fowls in plenty here;
> Scratch them, make their feathers fly,
> Wring their necks until they die."

Out came Pussy-cat in an instant. What a confusion there was in the henhouse. Cluck-cluck-cluck went the hens, flying all over the place; but no use: Pussy got them all, and scratched out their feathers, and wrung their necks. Then she went back into Blackbird's ear, and Blackbird went to sleep.

When morning came, the King said to his men, "Go, fetch the carcass of that insolent bird, and give the Chickens an extra bushel of corn." But when they entered the henhouse, Blackbird was singing away merrily on the roost, and all the fowls lay around in heaps with their necks wrung.

They told the King, and an angry King was he. "To-night," said he, "you must shut up Blackbird in the stable." So Blackbird was shut up in the stable, among the wild Horses.

At midnight, when all the world was asleep, Blackbird said—

> "Come out, Rope, and come out, Stick,
> Tie the Horses lest they kick;
> Beat the Horses on the head,
> Beat them till they fall down dead."

Out came Club and Rope from Blackbird's ear; the Rope tied the horses, and the Club beat them, till they died. Then the Rope and the Club went back into the Blackbird's ear, and Blackbird went to sleep.

Next morning the King said—

"No doubt my wild Horses have settled the business of that Blackbird once for all. Just go and fetch out his corpse."

The servants went to the wild Horses' stable. There was Blackbird, sitting on the manger, and drumming away on his walnut-shell; and all round lay the dead bodies of the Horses, beaten to death.

If the King was angry before, he was furious now. His horses had cost a great deal of money; and to be tricked by a Blackbird is a poor joke.

The Valiant Blackbird

"All right," said the King, "I'll make sure work of it to-night. He shall be put with the Elephants."

When night came the Blackbird was shut up in the Elephants' shed. No sooner was all the world quiet, than Blackbird began to sing—

> "Come from out my ear, you Ants,
> Come and sting the Elephants;
> Sting their trunk, and sting their head,
> Sting them till they fall down dead."

Out came a swarm of Ants from the Blackbird's ear. They crawled up inside the Elephants' trunks, they burrowed into the Elephants' brains, and stung them so sharply that the Elephants all went mad, and died.

Next morning, as before, the King sent for the Blackbird's carcass; and, instead of finding his carcass, the servants found the Blackbird rub-a-dub-dubbing on his drum, and the dead Elephants piled all round him.

This time the King was fairly desperate. "I can't think how he does it," said he, "but I must find out. Tie him to-night to my bed, and we'll see."

So that night Blackbird was tied to the King's bed. In the middle of the night, the King (who had purposely kept awake) heard him sing—

> "Come out, River, from my ear,
> Flow about the bedroom here;
> Pour yourself upon the bed,
> Drown the King till he is dead."

Out came the River, pour-pour-pouring out of the

Blackbird's ear. It flooded the room, it floated the King's bed, the King began to get wet.

"In Heaven's name, General Blackbird," said the King, "take your wife, and begone."

So Blackbird received his wife again, and they lived happily ever after.

The Goat and the Hog

A GOAT and a Hog were great friends, and for a long time they lived together. But they were poor, and one day the Goat said to the Hog—

"Good-bye, friend Hog! I am going to seek my fortune."

"Ugh! ugh! ugh!" said the Hog. It was kindly meant, for that was all the ignorant Hog could say. He intended to bid good-bye to his friend, and to wish him good luck.

The Goat trotted along till he came to the nearest town. He found a grain-shop with nobody in it; so in went our Goat, and ate his fill of the Grain, and whatever he could find. Then he went into the inner room, and sat down.

By-and-by the shopman came in; his little girl was with him, and the little girl began to cry for sugar.

"Go and get some out of the cupboard," said the shopman.

The little girl ran into the inner room to get the sugar, but the Goat was there. And when the Goat saw the little girl, he cried out, in a solemn and loud voice—

"Little girl, go run, go run,
Or your life is nearly done!
And my crumpled horns I'll stick
Through your little body quick!"

The little girl ran out shrieking. "What is it, my dear?" said her father.

"A demon, father!" she said; "save me from his crumpled horn."

What a terrible thing to happen in a quiet household! The poor man did not know what to do. So he sent for all his relations, and they advised him to try what the parson could do.

So the Parson was sent for, and the Clerk, and the Sexton, with bell, book, and candle. They lit the candle, and opened the book (I think it was a Latin Grammar, which they judged would be enough to scare any demon), and rang the bell; and then the Parson, with his heart in his boots, advanced into the room.

Instantly a horrid groan burst upon his ears (or so he thought), and a deep voice said—

"Parson, fly! or I will poke
  This my crumpled horn into you!
You'll admit it is no joke
  When you feel its point go through you!
Sexton, dig his grave, and then
Let the Clerk reply, Amen!"

The Parson dropt his Latin Grammar, and ran away, nor did he stop until he was safe in his own church.

At this the Shopman went down on his knees, and put his hands together, and said—

"O most respectable Demon! whoever you are, I

The Goat and the Hog

pray you do me no harm; and I will worship you, and offer you anything you may desire."

Then the Goat came majestically out, walking upon his hind legs, with his grey beard flowing from his chin, and he said—

"Put wreaths and jewels about my neck, and on each of my horns, and round my paws and my tail, and give me sweetmeats to eat, and I will do you no harm."

The Shopman made haste to do all this; he wreathed the Goat with flowers, and put all his wife's jewels upon the horns and paws, and all the jewels he could borrow from his neighbours.

The Goat went home, and showed all this magnificence to his friend the Hog. The Hog winked his greedy little eyes, and somehow made his friend understand that he would like some too. Then the Goat told him how he got the things, and showed him the way to the place.

So the Hog went to the same shop, and found it empty. The Shopman and his little girl had gone out to tell all the town what adventures they had passed through. The Hog grubbed up all he could find to eat, and then went and sat in the inner room.

Soon the Shopman and his little girl came back. The little girl ran inside to take off her little hat, and what does she see but a big black Hog sitting there! The Hog remembered his lesson, and wanted to say some terrible thing as the Goat had done; but all he could get out was—

"Ugh! ugh! ugh!"

This did not frighten the little girl at all. She ran out to her father, saying—

"O papa! there is a big black Hog inside!"

The Shopman got out his knife, and whetted it on the grindstone, and then he went into the room.

"Ugh! ugh! ugh!" said the Hog.

The Shopman said nothing, but stuck his knife into the Hog. Then there was a squealing and squalling, if you like! But in two minutes the Hog was dead, and in two hours he was skinned and cut up, and by nightfall, the Shopman and his little girl, and all their friends, were sitting round a delicious leg of roast pork, and the Sexton rang the bell for dinner, and the Parson said grace, and the Clerk said Amen.

The Parrot and the Parson

THERE was once a Banker who taught his Parrot the speech of men. The Parrot made such progress that he was soon able to take part in any conversation, and he astonished every one by his intelligence.

One day a Parson came by the Parrot.

"My respects to your Reverence," said the Parrot.

The Parson looked all round him, he looked down at his feet, he looked up into the sky; but no one could he see who might have spoken to him. He could not make it out; he thought it must have been a ghost. Then the Parrot spoke again. "It was I who saluted you," said he. The Parrot was close to the Parson's ear, and now at length the Parson saw him. The Parrot went on—

"O reverend Sir, you teach men how to get free from the chains of their sins. May it please you to tell me how to escape from this cage?"

This was a practical question, but the Parson's advice was not usually asked on such points. He did not know what to say.

"I fear I can be of no use to you," said he, "but I will consult my Solicitor."

The Parson went to see his Solicitor, and paid him six and eightpence. He might have bought the Parrot, cage and all, for half that; but, as I said, he was not a practical man. When he told the Solicitor what business he came about, the Solicitor said nothing at all, but fell down in a faint.

"What can I have said to make him faint?" the Parson thought. "Perhaps it is the hot weather." He poured water over the Solicitor's face, and by-and-by the Solicitor came to.

The Parson was much distressed at having thrown away six and eightpence; but he knew it would be of no use asking the Solicitor to give any of it back, so he did not try. He went back to the Parrot and said—

"Dearly beloved bird, I much regret having no information to give you which may be of use. The fact is, no sooner did I put your question to my worthy Solicitor, than he fell down in a dead faint."

"Oh," said the Parrot, "many thanks, Parson."

The Parson went away to the parish meeting. When he had gone, the Parrot stretched himself out on the bottom of his cage, and shut his eyes, and cocked up his feet in the air.

By-and-by the Banker came in, and saw his Parrot lying on his back, with his feet pointing to the sky.

"Poor Poll," said he, "you're dead, my pretty Poll."

The Parrot and the Parson

He opened the door of the cage, and took
out the bird, and laid him on the
ground. Immediately the Parrot
opened his wings and
flew away.

The Lion and the Hare

ONCE upon a time there was a Lion, who used daily to devour one of the beasts of the forest. They had to come up one after another, when called for. At last it came to the Hare's turn to be eaten, and he did not want to be eaten at all. He lingered and he dallied, and when at last he plucked up courage to come, he was very late. The Lion, when he saw the Hare coming, bounded towards him. The Hare said—

"Uncle Lion, I know I am late, and you have cause to be angry. But really it is not my fault. There is another Lion in our part of the jungle, and he says that he is master, and you are nobody. In fact, when I showed him that I positively would come to you he was very angry."

"Ha!" said the Lion, roaring; "who says he is my master? Show him to me. I'll teach him who rules the forest."

"Come along then," said the Hare.

They went a long way, until they came to a well. The Hare looked down into the well. "He was here just now," said he.

The Lion and the Hare

The Lion looked in, and at the bottom he saw what looked like a Lion in the water. He shook his mane—the other Lion shook his mane. He roared—the echo of a roar came up from the bottom of the well. "Let me get at him!" roared the Lion. In he jumped—splash! Nothing more was ever heard of that Lion, and the beasts of the forest were glad to be left in peace. They put their heads together, and composed a verse of poetry, which is always sung in that forest on Sundays:—

"The Hare is small, but by his wit
He now has got the best of it;
By folly down the Lion fell,
And lost his life within the well."

The Monkey's Bargains

ONCE upon a time an old Woman was cooking, and she ran short of fuel. She was so anxious to keep up her fire, that she tore out the hairs of her head, and threw them upon the flame instead of fuel.

A Monkey came capering by, and saw the old Woman at her fire.

"Old Woman," said the Monkey, "why are you burning your hair? Do you want to be bald?"

"O Monkey!" quoth the old Woman, "I have no fuel, and my fire will go out."

"Shall I get you some fuel, mother?" said the Monkey.

"That's like your kind heart," said the old Woman. "Do get me some fuel, and receive an old Woman's blessing."

The Monkey scampered away to the woods, and brought back a large bundle of sticks. The old Woman piled the dry sticks on the fire, and made a fine blaze. She put on her cooking-plank, and made four cakes.

All this while, the Monkey sat on his tail, and watched her. But when the cakes were done, and gave

The Monkey's Bargains

forth a delightful odour, the Monkey got up on his hind legs, and began dancing and cutting all manner of capers round about the cakes.

"O Monkey," said the old Woman, "why do you caper and dance around my cakes?"

"I gave you fuel," said the Monkey, "and won't you give me a cake?"

It seems to me that she might have thought of that without being asked; but she did not, so the Monkey had to ask for it.

Well, the old Woman gave the Monkey one cake, and the Monkey took his cake in high glee, and capered away.

On the way, he passed by the house of a Potter; and at the door of the Potter's house sat the Potter's son, crying his eyes out.

"What is the matter, little boy?" asked the Monkey.

"I am very hungry," whimpered the Potter's son, "and I have nothing to eat."

"Will a cake be of any use?" asked the kind Monkey.

The Potter's little Boy stretched out his hand, and into his hand the Monkey put his cake. Then the little Boy stopped crying, and ate the cake, but he forgot to say thank you. Perhaps he had never been taught manners, but the Monkey felt sad, because that was not the kind of thing he was used to.

The Potter's little Boy then went into the shop, and brought out four little earthenware pots, and began to play with them. He took no more notice of the Monkey, now that he had eaten his cake; but when the Monkey saw these earthenware pots, he began to dance and cut capers round them, like mad.

"Why are you dancing round my pots?" asked the little Boy. "Are you going to break them, Monkey?"

The Monkey replied, capering about all the while—

> "One old Woman, in a fix,
> Made me go and gather sticks;
> Then she gave me, for the sake
> Of the fuel, one sweet cake.
> That sweet cake to you I gave:
> In return, one pot I crave."

The Potter's little Boy was very much afraid of this dancing and singing Monkey, and perhaps he was a little bit ashamed of his ingratitude; so he gave the Monkey one of his four pots.

Away capered the Monkey, in high glee, carrying his pot. By-and-by he came to a place, where was a Cowherd's wife making curds in a mortar.

"What an odd thing to do, Mrs. Cowherd," said the Monkey. "Have you a fancy for making curds in a mortar?"

"No," said the Cowherd's wife, "but I have nothing better to make my curds in."

"Here's a pot which will do better than a mortar to make curds in," said the Monkey, offering the pot which he had received from the little Boy.

"Thank you, kind Mr. Monkey," said the Cowherd's wife. She took the pot and made curds in it. She took out the curds from the pot, and put them ready for eating, and some butter beside them. The Monkey watched her, sitting upon his tail.

Then the Monkey got up off his tail, and began to dance and cut capers round the curds and the butter.

"Why are you dancing about my butter?" said the Cowherd's wife. "Do you want to spoil it?"

Then the Monkey began to sing, as he capered about—

> "One old Woman, in a fix,
> Made me go and gather sticks;
> Then she gave me, for the sake
> Of the fuel, one sweet cake.
> Potter's son ate that, and he
> Gave a pot instead to me.
> Since to you I gave that pot,
> Give me butter, will you not?"

The wife of the Cowherd was much pleased with this song, as she was fond of music. "If your kindness," said she, "had not already earned the butter, your pretty song would be worth it." Then she gave him a good lump of butter.

Off went the Monkey in high glee, capering along with the lump of butter wrapped up in a leaf. As he went, he came to another place, where a Cowherd was grazing his kine. The Cowherd was sitting down at that moment, and enjoying his dinner, which consisted of a hunk of dry bread.

"Why do you eat dry bread, Mr. Cowherd?" asked the Monkey. "Are you fasting?"

"I am eating dry bread," quoth the Cowherd, "because I have nothing to eat with it."

"What do you say to this?" said the Monkey, cutting a caper, and offering to the Cowherd his lump of butter, wrapped up in a leaf.

"Ah," said the Cowherd, "prime." Not another word said he, but spread the butter upon his dry bread, and set to, with much relish.

The Monkey sat on his tail, and watched the Cowherd eating his meal. When the meal was eaten, up jumped the Monkey, and began capering and dancing, hopping and skipping, round and round the herd of kine.

"Ah," said the Bumpkin, "what are you a-doing that for?" The Bumpkin was so ignorant that he thought the Monkey wanted to bewitch his cattle, and dry up all their milk.

The Monkey went on with his skips and capers, and as he capered, he sang this ditty:—

> "One old Woman, in a fix,
> Made me go and get her sticks;
> Then she gave me, for the sake
> Of the fuel, one sweet cake.
> Potter's son the sweet cake got,
> Gave me, in return, one pot.
> Cow-wife had the pot, and she
> Butter gave instead to me.
> This I gave to you just now:
> Will you give me, please, one cow?"

"Ah," said the Bumpkin, "'spose I must." He was afraid of the Monkey's spells, and so he gave him a cow.

Away capered the Monkey, in high glee, leading his cow by a string. "I am indeed getting on in the world," said he.

By-and-by, what should he see coming along the road, but the King himself. The King was fastened to the shafts of a cart, which he was slowly dragging along; and jogging by the side of this cart was an ox; and upon the ox sat the Queen. This King had very simple tastes, and so had the Queen.

The Monkey's Bargains

"O King," said the Monkey, "why are you dragging your cart with your own royal hands?"

"This is the reason, O Monkey!" said the King. "My ox died in the forest, and I drag the cart because this cart will not drag itself."

"Come, sire," said the Monkey, "I don't like to see a King doing draught-work. Take this cow of mine, and welcome."

"Thank you, good and faithful Monkey," said the King. He mopped his brow, and yoked in the cow.

The Monkey began to dance and caper, jump and skip, round the Queen.

"What is the matter, worthy Monkey?" asked the King.

The Monkey began his ditty:—

> "One old Woman, in a fix,
> Made me go and gather sticks;
> Then she gave me, for the sake
> Of the fuel, one sweet cake.
> Potter's son the sweet cake got,
> Gave me in its place, one pot.
> Cow-wife had the pot, and she
> Butter gave instead to me.
> Bumpkin ate the butter, then
> Paid me with this cow again.
> Keep the cow, but don't be mean:
> All I ask for, is the Queen."

This seemed reasonable enough, so the King gave his Queen to the Monkey.

Away went the Monkey, capering along, and the Queen walked after (you see the King could not part with his ox as well as the Queen).

By-and-by they came to a Man sewing a button on to his shirt.

"Why, Man," said the Monkey, "why do you sew on your own buttons?"

"Because my wife is dead," said the Man.

"Here is a nice wife for you," said the Monkey. He gave the Queen to the Man. The Monkey then began his capers again, but all he could find to caper about, was a drum.

"You may have that drum, if you like," said the Man. "I only kept it because its voice reminded me of my wife, and now I have another."

"Thank you, thank you!" said the Monkey. "Now I am rich indeed!" Then he began to beat upon the drum, and sang:—

> "One old Woman, in a fix,
> Made me go and gather sticks;
> Then she gave me, for the sake
> Of the fuel, one sweet cake.
> Potter's son the sweet cake got,
> Gave me in its place, one pot.
> Cow-wife had the pot, and she
> Butter gave instead to me.
> Bumpkin ate the butter, then
> Gave a cow to me again.
> King took cow, but was not mean,
> For he paid me with a Queen.
> Now I have a drum, that's worth
> More than any drum on earth.
> You are worth a queen, my drum!
> Rub-a-dub-dub, dhum dhum dhum!"

So the Monkey capered away into the forest in high glee, beating upon his drum, and he has never been heard of since.

The Monkey's Rebuke

IN a certain village, whose name I know (but I think I will keep it to myself), in this village, I say, there was once a Milkman. I daresay you know that a Milkman is a man who sells milk; but I have seen milkmen who also sell water. That is to say, they put water in the milk which they sell, and so they get more money than they deserve. This was the sort of Milkman that my story tells of; and he was worse than the more part of such tricksters, since he actually filled his pans only half full of milk, and the other half all water. The people of that village were so simple and honest, that they never dreamt their Milkman was cheating them; and if the milk did seem thin, all they did was to shake their heads, and say, "What a lot of water the cows do drink this hot weather!"

By watering his milk, this Milkman got together a great deal of money: ten pounds it was, all in sixpences, because the villagers always bought sixpennyworth of milk a day.

When the Milkman had got ten pounds, that is to say, no less than four hundred silver sixpences, he thought he would go and try his tricks in another place, where there were more people to be cheated. So he put his four hundred silver sixpences in a bag, and set out.

After travelling a while, he came to a pond. He sat down by the pond to eat his breakfast, laying his bag of sixpences by his side; and after breakfast, he proceeded to wash his hands in the pond.

Now it so happened that this was the very pond where the Milkman came to water his milk. He came all this way out of the village, because he did not want to be seen by the people of the village. But there was one who saw him; and that was a Monkey, who lived in a tree which overhung the pond. Many a time and oft had this Monkey seen the Milkman pour water into the milk-cans, chuckling over the profit he was to make. This was a very worthy and well-educated Monkey, and he knew just as well as you or I know, that if you sell milk, you should put no water in it. When the Man stooped down to wash his hands in the pond, quietly, quietly down came the Monkey, swinging himself from branch to branch with his tail. Down he

L

The Monkey's Rebuke   143

came to the ground, and picked up the bag of sixpences, and then up again to his perch in the tree.

The Monkey untied the mouth of the bag, and took out one sixpence, and, click! dropped it into the pond. The Milkman heard a tiny splash, but it did not trouble him, because he thought it was a nut or something that had fallen from the tree. Click! another sixpence. Click! went a third.

By this time the Milkman's hands were dry, and he looked round to pick up his bag, and get him gone. But no bag! Click! click! went the sixpences all this while; and now the Milkman began to look around him. Before long he espied the Monkey sitting on a branch with his beloved bag, and—O horror! dropping sixpences, click! click! click! one after another into the pond.

"I say, you Monkey!" shouted he, "that's my bag! What are you doing? bring me back my bag!"

"Not yet," said the Monkey, and went on dropping the sixpences, click! click! click!

The Milkman wept, the Milkman tore handfuls of hair out of his head; but the Monkey might have been made of stone for all the notice he took of the Milkman.

At last the Monkey had dropt two hundred sixpences into the pond. Then he tied up the mouth of the money-bag, and threw it down to the Milkman. "There, take your money," said the Monkey.

"And where's the rest of my money?" asked the Milkman, fuming with rage.

"You have all the money that is yours," said the Monkey. "Half of the money was the price of water from this pond, so to the pond I gave it."

The Milkman felt very much ashamed of himself, and

went away, a sadder but a wiser man; and never again
did he put water in his milk. And that is why
I have not told you the name of the village
where he lived; for now that he has
turned over a new leaf, it would
hardly be fair to rake up
his old misdeeds
against him.

The Bull and the Bullfinch

UNDER a certain tree lived a wild Bull, and a Bullfinch had his nest in the branches. A Bull in a field is vicious enough, as I daresay you know; but a wild Bull is worse than anything. Wild Bulls are tremendously strong, and they can fight with almost any beast of the forest, even Lions and Tigers.

This wild Bull used to attack every creature that came near; and that, not for the sake of food, as Lions and Tigers do, but out of pure mischief. When the creature (were he man or beast) was killed, this wild Bull would leave the corpse lying, and begin to eat grass. But the little Bullfinch harmed nobody, unless it were a worm he would eat now and again for a treat. All day long he hopped about, picking up seeds, and singing away with all his throat. Many a time he saw the wild Bull gore some creature to death; and when he saw such things, tears would roll out of his eyes, because he could do nothing to help.

At last he thought to himself that he could at least warn the wild Bull of his wickedness, and clear his own conscience. So one morning, when the wild Bull was sitting under his tree, and looking around him, Bullfinch piped up, and said—

"Good brother Bull, I suppose we are akin somehow or other, because of our names."

"Yes, I daresay it may be so, Cousin Bullfinch," said the Bull.

"Well," says the Bullfinch, "allow me the right of a near kinsman to say something to you."

"All right, go ahead," said the Bull gruffly.

"Well," said the Bullfinch, clearing his throat (for he was a little frightened), "don't you know that murder is a very evil deed, and yet you do it every day of your life?"

"Impertinent speck!" said the Bull, getting up and walking away. He thought it cheeky that a bird so little should presume to rebuke a great big Bull. He did not remember, you see, that big bodies are often big fools, and precious goods are done up in small parcels. The warning of the little Finch was as the blowing of the wind; at least, so it seemed at the time, though afterwards (as you shall hear) the Bull did remember it.

So the Bull went on tossing and goring all that came within reach; and now he would have nothing to say to the poor little Bullfinch.

This went on, until one night a certain Lion had a dream. This Lion was King of the Forest, and he could conquer any creature who fought with him. In his dream the Lion thought that an angel stood before him, and said: "O Lion! in such a place, under a tree, lives a wild Bull, who does cruel murders every day upon innocent folk. By that tree is good pasture, and the wild Bull has grown very fat. I think he would make a nice meal for you; and at the same time you would be doing a good action in ridding the world of such a monster."

When day dawned, the Lion made no delay, but set out at once towards the place of the wild Bull. By-and-by he caught scent of the Bull, and then he uttered a terrible roar. The Bull heard the roar and was afraid; and still more feared he, when he saw this Lion approach, whom he knew to be the King of the Forest, and invincible.

"O Bull!" roared the Lion, "your hour has come. I am come to eat you, as a just punishment for your sins, and also because I am hungry."

At this the Bull trembled greatly, for he knew now that his sins had found him out. His knees gave way beneath him, and he was just about to sink to the ground, when the words of the Bullfinch came into his mind. Then he said—

"O mighty Lion! I have indeed deserved to be eaten, but I beg of you one last favour. Give me leave to bid farewell to a little kinsman of mine, Cousin Bullfinch, who lives in this tree, and at this moment is picking up seeds not far off."

The Lion was a good fellow, and had no wish to be hard on the Bull, so he said: "I give leave, O Bull, if you will promise on your honour to come back and be eaten."

The Bull gave his word that he would come back, and then went slowly away in search of the Bullfinch.

Master Bullfinch was at the moment eating his frugal breakfast of seeds. Suddenly he was aware that the wild Bull was approaching. He looked up, and seeing the dejected air of the Bull, he greeted him as cheerfully as he could, and then asked what the matter was? This Bullfinch bore no manner of grudge for the Bull's rudeness, because in his little body was a great heart, and he never thought of mean things.

"O Finchy, Finchy!" moaned the Bull, "look upon me for the last time! A hungry Lion has come to devour me, and it is of no use to resist; for he says that an angel has sent him to punish me for my sins."

"Poor old chap!" said the Bullfinch, "tell me all about it."

Then the wild Bull told him the dream which the Lion had seen.

"Ah," said the Bullfinch, "that is curious."

"Why?" asked the Bull.

"Because," said the Bullfinch, "I too had a dream last night, which I think the Lion ought to hear."

The wild Bull was not interested in the Bullfinch's dream; would you be interested in dreams, I wonder, if you expected to be eaten the next minute? However, he said nothing; and when Bullfinch fluttered his wings, and flew away towards the Lion, our friend the wild Bull followed slowly behind.

"Good morning, King Lion," said the little bird. "So you have had a dream?"

"Yes," said the Lion, and then he told the Bullfinch his dream.

"I had a dream too," said the Bullfinch, "and this it was. I dreamt that the same angel who came to you, came afterwards to me, and said, "O Bullfinch! when the Lion comes to eat your friend the Bull, tell him that he was sent not to destroy, but to cure; and that

The Bull and the Bullfinch

now the Bull repents of his evil ways, the Lion may go back again to his forest."

"Oh, I am so glad!" said the Lion. "I am hungry, it is true, but I daresay I can find some other creature, who has committed no sins, and wants no curing. So good-bye, friend Bull, and don't do it again." So saying, the Lion shook hands with both of them, and went to look for a fawn.

Then the Bull, wild no longer, thanked his friend the Bullfinch for saving his life, and they became faster friends that ever. The Bull gored no more creatures, indeed he welcomed them as his guests; and in the fat pastures around that tree you might have seen, if you had been there, whole herds of deer and antelopes grazing without any fear; and the Bull lived in their midst to a green old age, till he died respected and went to a happier world.

The Swan and the Crow

ONCE upon a time, two Swans had to leave home on account of a famine; and they settled by a lake in a distant land. By the side of this lake lived a Carrion Crow. The Swans built a nest, and Mrs. Swan laid two beautiful round eggs in the nest, and sat upon them. She had to sit on the eggs for weeks, in order to keep them warm, so that the little ones might grow up inside and be hatched. While she sat there, the Crow used to help Mr. Swan to find food for his wife; and when the cygnets came out of their shells, the Crow helped to feed them also.

So all went happily for a time, and Mr. and Mrs. Swan were deeply grateful to the kind Crow. But Crows are not kind without some reason, and what this Crow's reason was, you shall now hear.

Time went on, and one day Mr. Swan said to Mrs. Swan—

"My dear, the famine must be over by this time. What do you say? shall we go home again?"

"I am ready," Mrs. Swan said, "and we can start to-morrow if you like."

"Stop a bit," says Mr. Crow, "I have a word or two to say first."

"Why, what do you mean?" the Swans said, both together.

"I mean," said the Crow, "that you may go, if you like, but these cygnets are as much mine as yours, and may I be plucked if I let them go with you!"

"Yours!" said Mrs. Swan. "Who laid the eggs? who hatched them?"

"And who fed them, I should like to ask?" said the Crow, with a disagreeable laugh: "Caw, caw, caw!"

Here was a bolt from the blue! The Crow stuck to it, and the end of all was, that Mrs. Swan stayed behind to look after her little ones, while Mr. Swan flew off to lay a complaint in court against the greedy Crow.

But you must not suppose that this Crow meant to sit still, and let the Swan have things all his own way. Not he; off he flew secretly to the Judge, and to the Judge said he—

"O Judge, a Swan is going to lodge a false charge against me, and I want your help!"

"If it is false," said the Judge, "you want help from no one."

"Caw, caw, caw!" said the Crow, "you understand me." Then this vulgar Crow winked one eye at the Judge.

"Hm, hm," said the Judge, looking at the Crow. It is a pity to say it, but it is quite true, that this Judge was an unjust Judge; and he was ready to give any decision, right or wrong, so long as he was bribed well for his trouble. In that country, you see, there was no jury to decide matters, but all power lay in the hands of the Judge.

The Judge winked one eye at the Crow. Then he said, very softly, "What will you give me?"

"Silver and gold have I none," said the Crow, "but I'll tell you what I will do. I'll carry your father's bones to the Holy Land, and bury them in Jerusalem, and then your father will be sure to go to heaven."

The Judge was so foolish that he really believed his father would go to heaven at once, if only his bones were buried in Jerusalem, although his father had been as wicked as himself while he was alive. So he agreed to the Crow's proposal.

When the case came into court, of course the Judge gave decision in favour of the Crow, though there was no evidence on his side except his own word: and who but a fool would trust the word of a Carrion Crow? When the court rose, the Crow flew to the house of the Judge, and asked for the bones of the Judge's father. So the Judge tied up his father's bones in a bag, and hung the bag round the Crow's neck. Away flew the Crow, but he didn't fly far; for as the Judge watched him, the Crow hovered over a filthy drain; and untying the bag, began dropping the bones one by one into the mud.

"Hi, you brute!" shouted the Judge, "what are you doing!"

"Oh, you pumpkin!" said the Crow, "did you verily think that I should take the trouble to carry your father's rotten old bones to Jerusalem? No, no; I only wanted to see what rogues the race of Judges can be. Caw!" Flop! went the last bone into the mud, and away flew the Crow, and never came back there any more.

So the Judge had to pick his father's bones out of the gutter. And the next thing he had to do was to reverse his own decision, and give the Swan his

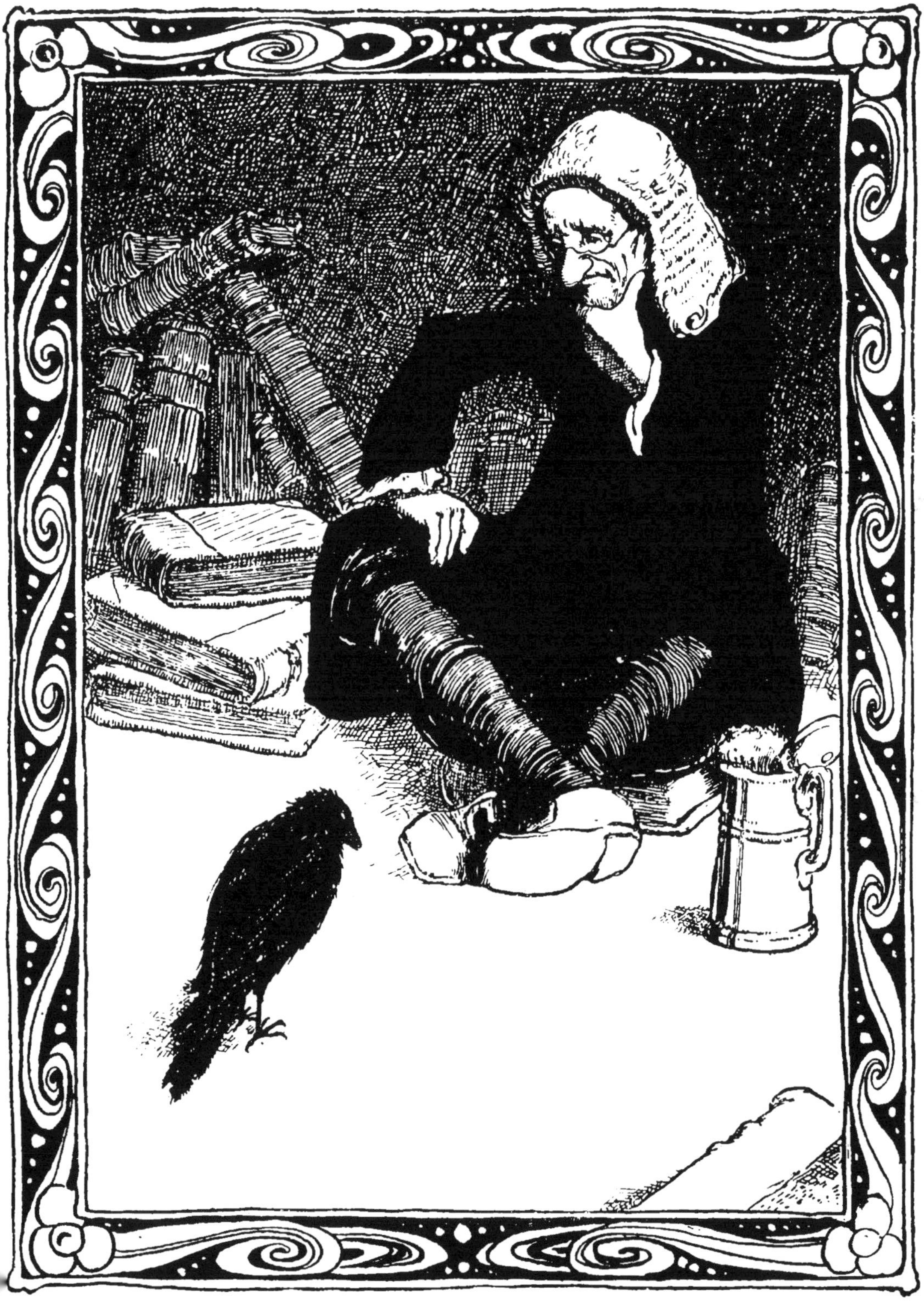

The Swan and the Crow

young ones again; because, you see, a great many people had heard what the Crow said to the Judge, and knew (if they didn't know it before) that the Judge was a rogue. So the Swan got his young ones back, and as for the Judge, he became the laughing-stock of the whole city, and he was obliged to go and try his tricks elsewhere.

Pride shall have a Fall

THERE was once a great drought in the land. For weeks and months not a drop of rain fell; and the sun beat down, and dried up the whole country, so that there was no water to be found. Now there was a certain pond in that country; and as day after day the sun blazed, the water sank lower and lower, until it was hardly an inch deep. Numbers of Frogs used to live in this pond; but as the water dried the Frogs died, so that the dry mud on the banks of the pond was covered all over with dead bodies of Frogs.

There came a Jackal out of the forest. He was glad to see this pool, because the pool where he used to drink had been quite dried up. So he made a little platform of mud, and stuck up four posts at the four corners; and then he gathered bundles of dry grass, and put them upon the top of the four posts for a thatch. Then his eye fell on the corpses of Frogs lying about; and being a foolish animal, he thought these corpses were uncommonly pretty. And what do you think he did? He gathered a lot of the dead Frogs and hung a fringe of them all round the thatch;

Pride shall have a Fall

and in each of his ears he hung a dead Frog, like an earring.

From far and near swarms of Rats used to come to this pond for drinking, since it was the only water to be found for a long distance, and all the rest was dried up. Then the Jackal kept guard over the pool; and not a drop might any Rat so much as taste, unless he would first bow down and worship the Jackal, and sing the following psalm, which the Jackal made up himself :—

> "A temple all of gold I found,
> With golden lamps hung all around;
> And see! the God himself is here,
> With two big pearls in either ear."

Even a Rat can tell a dead Frog from a pearl, but willy nilly he needs must sing it, or else no water. So when the Rat had sung this psalm, and bowed himself down three times before the Jackal, worshipping him as if he were a God, he was allowed to go down and take a sip of the water.

One day, what should come down to the water to drink but an Ox with one eye.

"Ho! ho! one-eyed Ox!" screamed the Jackal, "not a drop till you sing your psalm."

The Ox blinked his one eye stupidly, and looked round. "What psalm?" asked the one-eyed Ox.

"Mine," said the Jackal, who was very proud of his psalm, "my own composition." Then he sang it over to the Ox, that he might hear it.

> "'A temple all of gold I found—'

"That's this, you know," he explained, pointing to the scraggy thatch—

> "A temple all of gold I found,
> With golden lamps hung all around;
> And see! the God himself is here,
> With two big pearls in either ear."

"Ah," said the one-eyed Ox, "I'm rather stupid, I fear, and it will take me a minute or two to learn that psalm. It's a mighty fine psalm, that; I never heard the like in church. Suppose I say it over to myself while I'm a-drinking? that will save time, and it would be a thousand pities to spoil a thing like that."

This flattered the Jackal so much that he agreed.

One-eye went down to the pool, and took a long, long pull at the water. Then he came out of the water, and went slowly up to the Jackal, as he was sitting under his thatch, with its string of dead Frogs, and the two Frogs in the Jackal's ears.

"Now then, booby!" the Jackal said, "look sharp, the God is waiting."

The Ox opened a big mouth, and in a very hoarse voice he sang—

> "A nasty dirty thatch I found,
> With dried-up Frogs hung all around;
> And see! the mangy Jackal here,
> With two dead Frogs in either ear."

You may imagine the rage of the Jackal to hear this! He fairly foamed at the mouth. "You blasphemous beast!" screamed he, "I'll teach you to abuse a God!" And with that he jumped down off his seat, and gave chase.

Away scuttled the Ox; and as he ran, the water he had been drinking went gurgling inside him, flippity-flop, flippity-flop.

Pride shall have a Fall

This sound rather frightened the Jackal. "What's that?" he cried.

"A dog at your heels," said the Ox.

The Jackal was so scared at the very name of dog, that he turned about in no time, blind with terror, and away he scampered as hard as he could pelt.

He was so frightened, that he did not see where he was going; so he ran straight into the midst of a pack of hounds, who made short work of the conceited Jackal.

The Kid and the Tiger

A NANNY-GOAT and a Tigress were near neighbours in a certain wood, and fast friends to boot. The Tigress had two tiger-cubs; and the family of the Nanny-goat were four frolicksome kids, named Roley, Poley, Skipster, and Jumpster.

But the Tigress was jealous of her friend the Nanny-goat, because Nanny had four young ones, while she had only two. One day, as she was musing on the injustice of her fate, she thought to herself, "What if I eat up two of Nanny's kids, and then things will be equal? They do say, friends have all things in common." So to Nanny-goat she hied, and said she—

"Sister Nanny, my little ones have gone out, and I am very lonely at home. Do let one of your dear kiddies come and sleep with me, for company. Will you, please?"

"Gladly will I, sister," said honest Nanny-goat, thinking no evil of her friend. Then she ran out to the fields, where Roley and Poley were rolling over each other, and Jumpster was jumping over the back of Skipster.

"Children, children!" said Nanny-goat, "a treat for

The Kid and the Tiger

you! A kind friend has asked one of you out to spend the night."

"Baa baa baa!" cried the Kids, running up; and then three of them called out all together, dancing about old Nanny, "Let me go! Let me go! Let me go!" But the fourth, who was a wise little imp (and Roley it was, to be sure), asked in a quiet tone, "Who is it, Mammy Nanny-goat?"

"Why, who should it be but your Aunt Yellowstripe?" said Nanny.

At this they all looked rather crestfallen; for although Nanny-goat loved her friend dearly, all the youngsters were afraid of her, for what reason they could not say. Children have a way of finding out their friends; and these Kids had noticed at times a gleam in the eyes of Auntie Yellowstripe, which boded ill to little Kids.

"No-o, thank you, Mammy Nanny-goat," said Skipster, skipping away.

"No-o-o, thank you, Mammy," said Jumpster, and jumped after her.

"No-o-o-o, thank you," said Poley, and rolled away by himself.

Why did Poley roll away by himself? Because Roley stayed behind. Roley did not say No, thank you; on the contrary, he said Yes. Why Roley said yes instead of no, was his own concern; and I think Roley knew what he was about.

This was how Roley went with the Tigress; and that night the Tigress put him to sleep by her side. She cuddled him up, and made a great fuss of him, thinking to herself, "Soft words cost nothing; and when he is fast asleep, we shall see what we shall see."

But Roley was no such fool as the Tigress thought him. So he did not go to sleep, but only pretended; and no sooner did Dame Yellowstripe begin to snore, than up jumps Roley, as soft as you please, and fetches out one of Yellowstripe's own cubs, who were sleeping away at the back of the cave. He laid the cub in his own place, and went into the corner to sleep with the other cub.

About midnight the Tigress awoke, and as she felt the warm little thing nestling beside her, she chuckled to herself. Then she gave him one tap with her mighty paw; crack! went his neck, and his dancing days were over; the Tigress gobbled him up, skin, bones, and teeth. It was pitch dark, you know, and she could not see that she was eating her own cub. "One less of the brood now," thought the Tigress; turned over, and went to sleep again.

Next morning, they all woke up; and Yellowstripe, to her dismay, saw that Roley was rolling about, right as a trivet. She looked round for her own cubs, and lo and behold! one was missing. At first she could not make it out in the least; but when it dawned upon her what had happened, she nearly turned yellow all over with rage and disappointment.

"Did you have a good night, Roley dear?" said she in a wheedling tone to the Kid.

"Oh yes, Auntie," said the little Kid, "only a gnat bit me."

This astonished the Tigress, who thought that the Kid must be stronger than he appeared to be. "Never mind," said she to herself; "come to-night, we shall see what we shall see."

That night all went as before; only this time Roley put a huge stone in his place, and then he ran off as fast as his legs could carry him. When the Tigress awoke, she gave a pat to the stone: it hurt her paw sadly.

"Good heavens," said she, "what a mighty Kid it is, to be sure! I must make short work of him now I have the chance, or there is no knowing what may happen. When he grows up, he may kill me." So she gave a fierce bite at the stone, and broke all her front teeth.

Now the Tigress' fury knew no bounds. She went raging about the cave, hunting in every corner for Roley; but Roley was not to be found, because, as I have told you, he was not there. So the Tigress was forced to wait until morning for her revenge.

All night long the Tigress lay awake with the pain of her teeth; and when morning came, she sought out a familiar friend to take counsel with. This friend was an old one-eyed Tiger. The Tigress and the one-eyed Tiger talked for a long time together, and as they talked they walked. When they came to the end of their talk, their walk was also at an end, and they found themselves at the mouth of Yellowstripe's den. There in the den, as calm as you please, playing with the one remaining Tiger cub, was Roley.

"Ha ha," laughed One-eye, "so there you are. Let us sit down, and I will tell you a story."

"Do, do, Nuncle One-eye," cried Roley.

So they all sat down, and One-eye began. "When I eat little Kids," said One-eye, "four of them make me a mouthful; and I'm coming one of these days to make one mouthful of you and your brother and sisters."

"Capital, capital, Nuncle One-eye!" said Roley,

clapping his paws; "what good stories you do tell, Nuncle One-eye! Now I'll tell you a story. When you come to eat us up, Skipster will hold you by the forelegs, and Jumpster will hold you by the hind legs, and Poley will hold your head, and Roley will chop it off, if only mother will give us a light."

This terrified One-eye extremely, for he was a great coward. He thought it all as true as gospel, so he took to his heels, and left Yellowstripe in the lurch.

On the way, he met six other Tigers, friends of his. "Oh my friends!" said he, "I have such a treat for you! A fine fat Kid, crying out to be killed! Come along, come along, I'll show you the way, and all I ask is the pleasure of serving you." Cunning old One-eye!

The six Tigers believed all that One-eye said, and away they all trotted together towards the place where Roley lived. They knew he would go home sooner or later; and indeed he was there already, and saw them coming, so he climbed up a tree. Goats are wonderfully good at climbing rocks, but I think most of them cannot climb trees; still, whatever may be true of other goats, Roley could. If it were not so, this story would never have been written. So Roley climbed up a tree, and sat on a branch, with his legs all dangling in the air.

The first Tiger gave a jump, and missed him. Number two gave a jump, and missed him. They all jumped, one after another, and not one of them could touch Roley; who sat and laughed at them so heartily, that he nearly fell off his perch.

At last, when they were tired of jumping, and jumping, up gets old One-eye, and says, "I know how to get at him. I'll stand here, and you get on my back, and then

The Kid and the Tiger

the rest of you one a-top of another, and then we shall catch him nicely." They all thought this an excellent idea; so One-eye propped his old carcass against the tree, and the other Tigers mounted one on another's shoulders, until there they were, all seven in a pyramid. Then the topmost Tiger stretched out his paw, and all but got hold of Roley.

Thereupon One-eye cocked up his solitary eye, to see how things were going on up aloft; and seeing this, Roley called out—

"Mother, give me a lump of mud, and I'll hit the brute in his sound eye, and then we will finish him off."

When One-eye heard this, he gave a great start, and down toppled the whole seven in a heap, one a-top of the next, spitting and roaring and scratching. They were so much taken aback, that they imagined all sorts of powerful beasts to be fighting with them, when it was only their own selves, biting each other; and the end of all was, that as soon as the seven Tigers had each got his four legs to himself, off they went helter-skelter into the forest, and never more troubled Mammy Nanny-goat and her four frolicsome Kids.

The Stag, the Crow, and the Jackal

ONCE upon a time there was a Stag living in a certain jungle, and in the same jungle lived a Crow. These two were bosom friends. Why a Stag should take a fancy to a Crow, I cannot say; but so it was; and if you do not believe it, you had better not read any further.

It so befell that a Jackal came by one day, and his eye fell on this Stag, and a fine plump Stag he was. The Jackal's mouth began to water. How he would like to make a meal of so dainty a piece of flesh. But he knew it was of no use trying to attack the Stag, who seemed very strong. Still, by hook or by crook, that Stag he would have. So in the depths of his cunning heart he concocted a trick, of which you shall shortly hear.

The Jackal watched his chance, and as soon as he had found the Stag alone, he began to say, sidling up to the Stag, and whispering in his ear—

"Beware of that Crow; he's fooling thee. Beware, beware all birds of the air. There's no trusting any

The Stag, Crow, and Jackal

bird, let alone a Crow, who is worst of the whole feathered tribe. Now you and I, who never try in the air to fly, good honest gentlemen with four legs apiece, we are marked out for friends by Nature herself."

Will you be surprised to hear that the Stag listened to the crafty and slanderous words, and deserted his friend the Crow? When your hair is grey you will know that such is the way of the world, and that a true friend who sticks to the end, is harder to find than a diamond mine.

But although this Stag was shallow-hearted and weak, not so the Crow. He was a true friend, and he was cut to the heart by the unkindness of his friend the Stag; but he wasted no time in fruitless tears. He went about his work as usual, and waited for a chance of winning back his recreant friend.

Well, Stag and Jackal scoured about the woods together, and the Jackal did his best to make himself agreeable. In this he had poor success; for though the Stag tried hard to like his new comrade, yet he could not help seeing that he was dirty; moreover, the Jackal ate all sorts of dead animals, but the Stag was a vegetarian, and did not approve of this kind of food. But though the Stag had qualms now and again, he was not strong enough to break loose from the friendship of the Jackal.

But the time was ripening for the Jackal's blow. He knew a place where huntsmen used to set gins and snares, to catch the wild animals. So one day, as he and the Stag were out a-walking together, the Jackal so managed that they passed by this place. The

Jackal took good care to keep clear of the snare; but the innocent Stag knew nothing of snares or gins, so into a snare he stept, and snap! he was fast.

Now was the time for a true friend to show his friendship. But the Jackal, as we already know, was a humbug; accordingly, all he did was to sit by the side of the Stag, and try not to look pleased.

"Oh dear, what shall I do?" said the Stag, when he found himself caught. "Oh my friend, do help me out."

"You shock me, friend," said the Jackal, pulling a long face; "surely you have not forgotten that it is Sunday? We are told in the Ten Commandments to do no work on the Sabbath day. If it were not so, how gladly would I help you!" So saying, he wiped away a crocodile tear. He sat down and waited in the hope that the Stag would die, and then he would eat him.

But the faithful Crow was not far. Though his friend the Stag would not so much as cast him a look, the Crow followed him ever, biding his time; and now the time had come.

The Crow perched on a neighbouring tree, and said—

"Dear friend, I am only a weak little bird, and I cannot help you; but I can teach you to help yourself. My advice is, pretend to be dead, and when the Hunter comes, he will open the snare without any care, and you can escape."

"Thank you, long-suffering friend!" said the Stag; and so he did. When the Huntsman came, he thought the Stag was dead; he opened the snare,

The Stag, Crow, and Jackal

and before he was aware, the Stag was up and off and away.

The Stag asked his friend the Crow to forgive him, and they lived happily together as before. As for the treacherous Jackal, he never came near them more.

The Monkey and the Crows

IN a certain land, a flock of Crows built their nests in the branches of a huge cotton-tree.

In that country, the climate is not the least like ours. It is hot all the year round, and for eight months the sun blazes like a fiery furnace, so that the people who live there are burnt as black as your boot; then after eight months comes the rain, and the rain comes down in bucketsful, with lightning fit to blind you, and thunder enough to crack your head. These Crows were quite happy in their nests, whatever happened; for when it was hot, the leaves of the trees sheltered them from the sun, and in the rainy season the leaves kept them pretty dry.

One evening there came a terrible storm, with torrents of rain like Noah's flood. In the midst of it, the Crows noticed a Monkey sliding along, drenched and draggle-tailed, looking like a drowned Rat. The Crows set up a chorus of caws, and called out—

"O Monkey, what a fool you must be! Look at us, dry and comfortable, in our nests of rags and twigs. If we, with only our little beaks to help us, can make

The Monkey and the Crows

comfortable nests, why can't you, with two hands and two feet and a tail?"

You might have thought the Monkey would take this advice to heart. But not a bit of it. Monkeys are naturally a lazy tribe, and they are full of envy, hatred, and malice. What they like best is destroying whatever they can lay their hands on; and when I look upon some of the nations of this globe, I cannot help thinking that they really must be descended from Monkeys. So this Monkey snapt and snarled, and said to the Crows—

"Just wait till morning, and then we'll see what a Monkey can do."

The simple birds were delighted to hear this, and looked forward to seeing the Monkey do something wonderfully clever, with his tail and his two hands and two feet.

Morning came, and the rain was over. The Monkey climbed up into the tree, and in his rage and envy he tore all the Crows' nests to pieces.

The Monkey and the Crows

Then the Crows were sorry they spoke, and determined for the future to mind their own business, and let fools alone. For, as the wise man said, "To give good advice to a fool is like pouring oil upon the fire."

The Swan and the Paddy-Bird

A WILD Swan was flying once to his home, when he paused to rest on a tree. This was a kind of tree you have most likely never seen. It was very tall, and had no branches upon it until you came to the top, but at the top was a large clump of green leaves, and bunches of cocoa-nuts hanging down.

It so happened that on this tree was the nest of a Paddy-bird. A Paddy-bird is a bird something like a heron, which feeds on fish and frogs. At the moment when the Swan perched upon the tree, this Paddy-bird was sitting demurely on the edge of a pond that was below the tree, watching the water for a rise. She had no fishing-rod, but when she saw a little fish or a frog swim past, out went her beak like a flash, and the fish was pierced. Then she ate the fish, or carried it off to her little ones in the nest.

When the Paddy-bird chanced to look round, she saw the Swan sitting upon her tree. She was frightened at this, thinking that perhaps it was some bird of prey, come to devour her chicks. So she left her fishing, and at once flew up to the top of the cocoa-nut tree. The Swan looked harmless enough when she came closer, so plucking up courage, the Paddy-bird thus addressed him—

"Good-day, sir. May I ask who you are?"

"I am a Swan," said the other, "and I am on my way home; but as it is a hot day, I thought I would rest awhile on your tree. I hope you have no objection?"

"Welcome, my lord Swan, welcome!" said the Paddy-bird. "I only wish I could offer you entertainment. But I am ashamed to say that I have no food worth your taking. I am a poor bird, and you know we Paddy-birds eat only small fish and frogs, which your highness would hardly touch."

"Oh, never mind for that," answered the Swan; "thank you all the same, but I can find my own food on this tree of yours."

This set our Paddy-bird's heart all a-flutter, for what could he mean but her brood? However, all was well in a minute; when she saw the Swan go to one of the green cocoa-nuts hanging to the tree. You have seen, I suppose, three little soft places at the top of a cocoa-nut, which are holes in the shell filled up with pulp. The Swan pierced his bill through one of these holes, and drank the milk inside the cocoa-nut. Then he gave some of the milk to the Paddy-bird, and flew away.

This milk tasted very nice, and the Paddy-bird began to say to herself, "What a fool I have been all these years! Here am I, watching and waiting all day long for a frog, and nasty things they are too, and all this while there was plenty of delicious milk within a yard of my nest! Well, good-bye fish, and good-bye frogs; I have done with you now for ever."

The Swan and the Paddy-bird

The next time the Paddy-bird felt hungry, she flew to a cocoa-nut and began to peck at it. But she did not know the secret of the three little holes at the top of the cocoa-nut; so she pecked, and pecked, and got no further. At last she gathered all her strength, and gave a tremendous peck at the cocoa-nut. Snap! her bill broke off, and the blood ran out, and very soon the poor Paddy-bird had bled to death.

Next day, the Swan happened to fly by that way again; and coming to the tree, he found his friend the Paddy-bird lying dead on the ground, with her bill snapt off clean. He understood at once what had happened, and said to himself, "This is what comes of trying to do what one is not fit for. Let the cobbler stick to his last, or misfortune follows fast."

What is a Man?

IN a certain forest, a Lioness dwelt who had one cub. This cub did not go to school, as you one day will go; but he learned his lessons at home. And what do you think his lessons were? Not multiplication which is vexation; not the Rule of Three which puzzles me; not spelling and copy-books. No; the Lioness had only one lesson to teach her cub, and that was, to avoid mankind as if they were poison. Every day, morning and evening, she taught him for an hour; telling him again and again, that of all the beasts of the forest he need fear none, for a lion is stronger than any, but man he must fear and keep clear of.

Well, the little Lion grew big; and as often happens to children as well as lions' cubs, he grew conceited too. He could not believe that his mother was old enough to know better than he; no, he would see for himself. So one fine day, this Lion set out on a voyage of discovery.

The first thing he saw was an Ox. This Ox was a fine sturdy animal, and the Lion felt rather nervous to see such hoofs and horns. You must remember he was young and ignorant, and had hardly seen any animal but his mother and father. So he went up to the Ox, and said timidly—

"Good morning, sir. Will you be good enough to tell me if you are a Man?"

If an Ox could laugh, that Ox would have laughed in the face of the Lion's cub. But an Ox is always solemn, like a Turk, though he does not love bloodshed as a Turk does. This Ox was chewing the cud, munching and mouthing with great calmness, so as to get the full flavour of the rich grass. He turned his meek eyes, and stared at the Lion. Then he said—

"A Man! God forbid. A Man is a terrible creature. He makes slaves of us Oxen, and puts a yoke on our necks and fastens us to a thing called a plough; and makes us pull the plough to and fro, up and down, till we are tired to death. If we won't go, he sticks a prod into us, which hurts us very much. I can't think what is the use of all this pother; we get no good of it. And when we are old, and can work no more, he kills us, and eats our flesh, and the skin he makes into shoes for his own feet. Keep clear of Men, if you value your life." Then the Ox turned his head away, and went on with his chewing.

This gave our Lion something to think about. He thought the Ox a very fine animal indeed, and yet, said the Ox, Man was stronger.

The Lion went his ways, and by-and-by, what should he see but a Camel. If the Ox was a fine creature, here was a finer; ever so tall, with a hump on his back, and a long neck, and great long legs. Surely this must be the terrible Man he had heard so much of. But to make certain, he approached the Camel with great respect, and said—

"Good morning, sir. Pray, will you tell me if you are a Man?"

The Camel turned his long neck, and sniffed and sneered as Camels have a way of doing, and a most unpleasant way it is.

"Pooh!" said he. "Stuff! poof! you oaf! you think me a Man? I wish I were a Man, wouldn't I make short work of you! A man, quotha! Why, I am a slave to that same Man. They catch us, these Men, and make a hole in our noses, and put a ring in it—do you see my ring? How do you think I like a hole made in my nose, as if two holes were not enough! Then they tie a rope to the ring, and lead us about all day long just where they please, without a with your leave, or by your leave! And they make us squat down in the mud, and put a great load on our backs, enough to crush a whipper-snapper like you. Groan as we may, it's all of no use, they do what they choose. Man! the very name makes me shiver. Get out, and leave me alone!"

This frightened our Lion, because who knew whether the great animal might not kill him, if it came into his head, so the Lion went away as fast as he could.

In a little while, he espied an Elephant. Here was a monster, to be sure! A great black mountain, with a long nose curling about, and huge white teeth sticking out, and big ears flapping. The Lion was quite terrified this time, and would not go near the Elephant, until he suddenly saw that the Elephant had a rope round his tusks, by which he was tied fast to a stake. Then he plucked up courage to approach, and said—

"Good morning, my lord. Please will you tell me, are you a Man?"

The Elephant trumpeted loudly. That was his way of laughing at the idea that he could be mistaken for a Man.

"Hooroo! hooroo!" he shrieked. "A Man! Hooroo! No, but a Man is my master, and that's the truth. A Man tied me to this post. Cruel and selfish brutes, are men; and with all my strength, I am no match for a Man. They get on our backs, a dozen of them at a time, and make us fetch, and carry, and drive us about by sticking a sharp spike into our skulls. Don't you go near a Man, if you love your life; why, bless me, they will make mincemeat of you! Hooroo!" The Elephant swished his trunk all round him in his excitement.

Our Lion had now seen three astonishing creatures, and they all said that a Man was stronger than they were. What could this terrible creature be like? He must be a mountain indeed, if he was to master such a beast as the black Elephant. Yet the black creature said that Men got on his back, a dozen of them at a time. The Lion could not understand it at all. He shook his head, and stalked away thoughtful.

As the Lion was going along, he saw a puny and weak-looking thing, walking upright on two legs. He seemed to be a kind of monkey, thought the Lion. It never entered his head that this little thing could be a Man, but he trotted up to him gaily, and said—

"Good morning, my friend. Can you tell me where

I can find a Man? I have been hunting for one all the morning."

"I am a Man," said the other.

At this the Lion laughed in his face. "You a Man!" said he. "Come, come; I may be young, but I am no fool, my good fellow. Why, you are not so big as one leg of that mountain over there, who was tied to a stake, as he said, by a Man."

"All the same," the Man said, "I am one of them."

"But look here," the Lion went on, "my father and mother both say that Man is a terrible and cruel creature, and the only creature a Lion need fear. Now, either you are no Man, or else my father and mother are quite wrong."

"Well," said the Man, "I am not nearly so strong as you are, or the Elephant and Camel, or even the Ox. As you say, I am not much to look at, but I have one power which you all lack."

"Indeed," said the Lion, "and what may that be?"

The Man answered, "Reason."

"I never heard of reason," said the Lion. "Please explain it to me, will you?"

What is a Man?

"It is not easy to explain what reason is," replied the Man; "but if you like, I will show you how it works."

The Lion was pleased. "Oh please do," he said.

I must tell you that this Man was a woodcutter, and he had an axe upon his shoulder. He now lifted this axe and drove a blow into a stout sapling which grew hard by. When he had split the sapling, he took a wedge of wood, and hammered it in with the back of his axe, until there was a large cleft in the trunk of the sapling. "Now then," said the Man, "just put your paw in that hole."

The Lion obediently put his paw into the cleft, and then the Man pulled out the wedge from the cleft. The sapling closed tight on the paw of the Lion, and squeezed it. "Now," said the Man, "you know what reason is."

But the Lion no longer cared to hear about reason; all he wanted was to get his paw out of the cleft. He pulled and he tugged, he roared and he struggled; but all of no use; he could not by any means get his paw free. The end of all was, in madness and fury he dashed his head against the ground, and died.

This was how the Lion learnt how terrible a being is Man; but unluckily, you see, his knowledge was of no use to him or any one else, because it cost him his life. If he had listened to his mother's teaching, he might be living still, and you would not be reading this story.

The Wound and the Scar

THERE was once a forest where a Lion dwelt. Over all the beasts of the forest the Lion lorded it, and of men not one durst come near the place for fear of King Lion; none, that is, except one only, a Woodman who lived in a little hut just upon the borders of the woodland; and between the forest and the hut a river flowed. This Woodman came often into the forest, to cut wood; and he had no fear to do so, because the Lion and he were bosom friends. Such fast friends they were that if ever the Woodman failed to pay his daily visit, the Lion was grieved and missed him sorely.

It happened once that the Woodman fell ill of a fever. In his woodland hut he lay all alone, for no wife was there, or sister to care for him. So he tossed and moaned, and waited for the hours to pass.

Of course during all this time the Woodman could not visit the forest, and his friend the Lion missed him. "What can be the matter," thought King Lion. "Has some enemy killed him, or has he fallen sick?" At last

The Wound and the Scar

he could no longer bear the suspense, and set out in search of the Woodman.

I do not think that the Lion had ever yet been to his friend's house; and for all he knew he might be walking straight into a trap. But he was so fond of the Woodman that he never thought of danger. All he wanted was to see his friend. Accordingly, he followed the path by which the Woodman came into the woods; and in due time this path led him to the bank of a wide and swift river, and over on the opposite bank was a hut.

In plunged the Lion, not waiting to think; and though there were crocodiles in that river ready to eat him, and though the current bade fair to sweep him away, so strong was his love for his friend that he swam across.

The Woodman's house stood within an enclosure, and all the doors and gates were shut; but the Lion jumped over the wall, and searched about, until he managed somehow to force his way into the house. Then he saw his friend lying upon a bed, and very ill, all alone, with no one to tend him.

How grieved the Lion was to see his friend, you can imagine better than I can tell. The Lion knelt down by his friend's side, and began to lick him all over. This woke the man from his dazed condition; and when he found the Lion licking his body, he did not like the smell of the Lion, so he turned his head away, with a grunt of disgust.

Now I think this was very unkind, because the Lion had no other way of showing how much he cared for his friend. Think what a long way he had come to see his friend, and think what danger he had faced; and now to be met with a grunt of disgust! The Lion stopped licking the Woodman, and got up slowly, and went away. Back he swam over the deep and swift river, but all the heart was taken out of him; he cared not for the crocodiles, indeed now he would not have been very sorry if a crocodile had devoured him. One crocodile did actually get a nip at his leg, and left a wound there. Back to his den he crept, solitary and sad. And when he got to his den, he lay down, sick of his friend's fever, which he had taken by licking him.

In a week or so, the Woodman was well again; and thinking nothing of what had passed, he shouldered his axe, and trudged away to cut wood. When the time came for his midday meal, he went as his custom was to the Lion's den; and there he found his friend the Lion, thin and sick.

"Why, friend, what is the matter?" the Woodman asked.

"I am ill," said the Lion.

"What is it?" asked the Woodman again.

But the Lion would answer nothing; and do what he would, the man could not get him to say another word. So he left him for that day, and went home.

For several days after, the man did the same thing; and gradually the Lion got better. At last one day, when the Lion was quite well again, the man said to him—

"Tell me, good friend Lion, what it is that has made you so silent and gloomy of late?"

Then answered the Lion, "O Woodman, I will tell

The Wound and the Scar

you. When you were ill, I swam a swift river and faced death, all for your sake; I came into your house when you lay deserted, and licked your body, and took the fever which you had into my veins; and this wound which you see, I received from a crocodile as I was swimming across on my way back. But you received me with scorn, and turned away your face in disgust. The fever is gone, and this wound (as you see) is healed; but the wound in my heart can never heal. You are no true friend; and from henceforth our ways lie apart."

The man was ashamed of his unkindness, but it was too late, for, as the poet says—

> "Who snaps the thread of friendship, never more
> Can join it as it once was joined before."

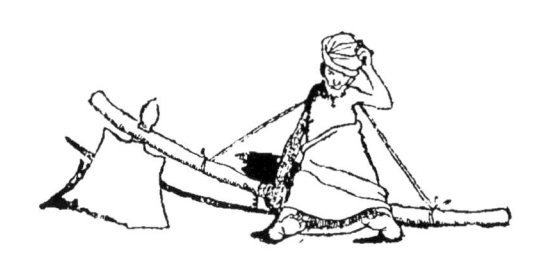

The Cat and the Parrot

ONCE upon a time, a Cat and a Parrot had joint lease of a certain piece of land, which they tilled together.

One day the Cat said to the Parrot, "Come, friend, let us go to the field."

Said the Parrot, "I can't come now, because I am whetting my bill on the branch of a mango-tree."

So the Cat went alone, and ploughed the field. When the field was ploughed, the Cat came to the Parrot again, and said—

"Come, friend, let us sow the corn."

Said the Parrot, "I can't come now, because I am whetting my beak on the branch of a mango-tree."

So the Cat went alone, and sowed the corn. The corn took root, the corn sprouted, it put forth the blade, and the ear, and the ripe corn in the ear. Then again the Cat came to the Parrot, and said—

"Come, friend, let us go and gather the harvest."

Said the Parrot, "I can't come now, because I am whetting my beak on the branch of a mango-tree."

So the Cat went alone, and gathered the harvest. She put it away in barns, and made ready for threshing.

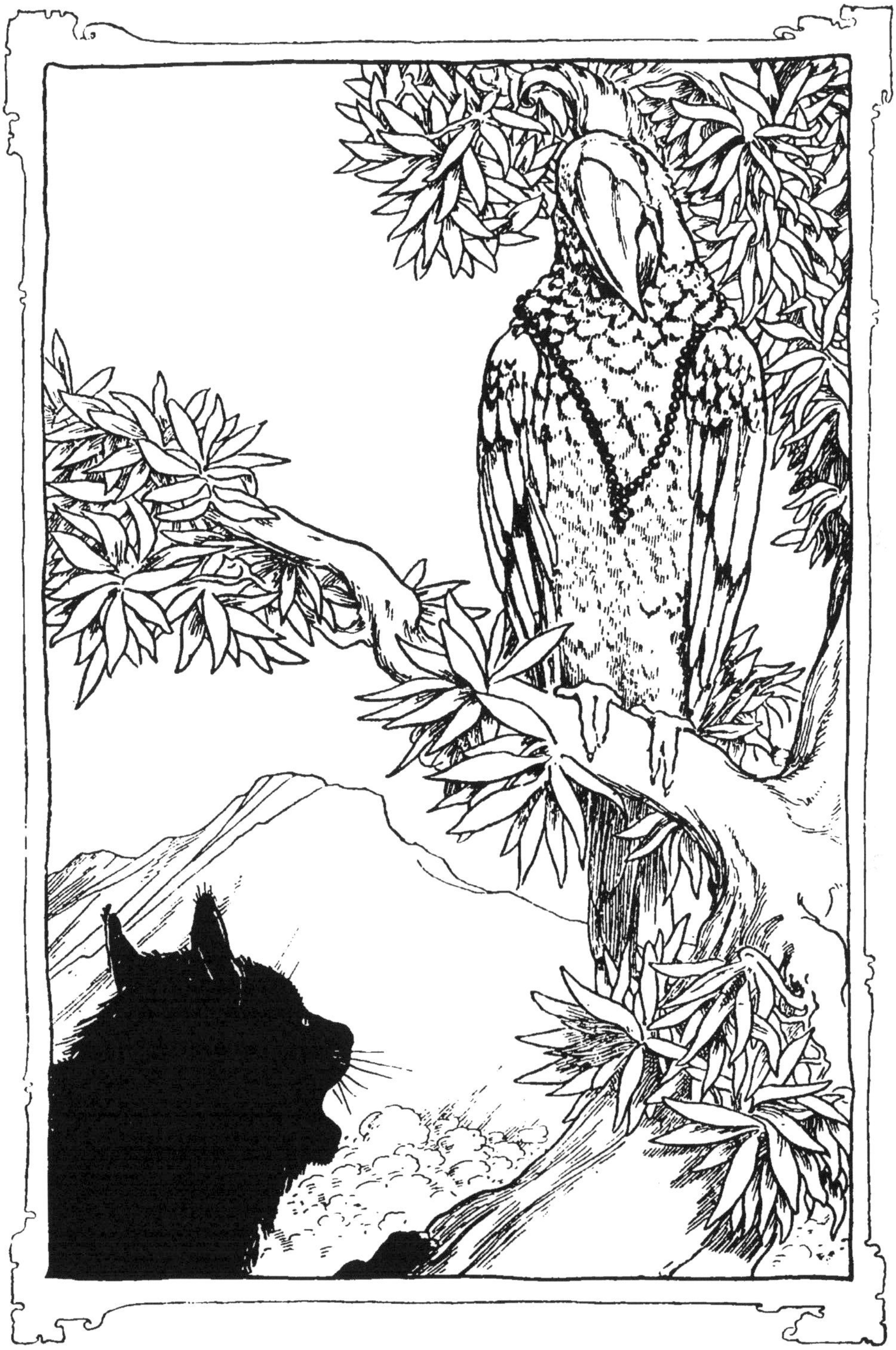

The Cat and the Parrot

When all was ready for the threshing, again the Cat came to the Parrot, and said—

"Come, friend, let us thresh the corn."

Said the Parrot, "I can't come now, because I am whetting my beak on the branch of a mango-tree."

So the Cat went, and threshed all the corn alone. Then the Cat came back to the Parrot, and said—

"Come, friend, let us go and winnow the grain from the chaff."

Said the Parrot, "I can't come now, because I am whetting my beak on the branch of a mango-tree."

So the Cat winnowed the grain from the chaff alone. Then she came back once again to the Parrot, and said—

"Come, friend, the grain is all winnowed and sifted; come and divide it between us."

"Certainly," said the Parrot, and came at once. You see the Cat had done all the work, but the Parrot was quite ready to share the profit. They divided the corn into two halves, and the Cat put her half away somewhere, and the Parrot carried his half to his nest.

Then the Cat and the Parrot agreed to invite each other to dinner every day; that is to say, the Cat asks the Parrot to-day, and the Parrot asks the Cat to-morrow. The Cat's turn came first. Then the Cat went to market and bought a ha'porth of milk, a ha'porth of sugar, and a ha'porth of rice. When the Parrot came there was nothing but this stingy fare. Moreover, the Cat was so inhospitable, that she actually made the Parrot cook the food himself! Perhaps that was her way of rebuking her friend for his laziness.

Next day the turn came to the Parrot. He procured

about thirty pounds of flour, and plenty of butter, and everything else that was needed, and cooked the food before his guest came. He made enough cakes to fill a washerwoman's basket—about five hundred.

When the Cat came, the Parrot put before her four hundred and ninety-eight cakes, in a heap, and kept back for himself only two. The Cat ate up the four hundred and ninety-eight cakes in about three minutes, and then asked for more.

The Parrot set before her the two cakes he had kept for himself. The Cat devoured them, and then asked for more.

The Parrot said, "I have no more cakes, but if you are still hungry, you may eat me."

The Cat was still hungry, and ate the Parrot, bones and beak and feathers. Thus the tables were turned; for if the Parrot had the best of it before, the Cat had the best of it now.

An old woman happened to be near, and saw this. So she picked up a stone, and said—

"Shoo! shoo! get away, or I'll kill you with this stone."

Now the Cat thought to herself, "I ate a basketful of cakes, I ate my friend the Parrot, and shall I blush to eat this old hag?"

No, surely not. The Cat devoured the old Woman.

The Cat went along the road and perceived a Washerman with a donkey. He said, "O Cat, get away, or my donkey shall kick you to death!"

Thought the Cat, "I ate a basketful of cakes, I ate my friend the Parrot, I ate the abusive old Woman, and shall I blush to eat a Washerman?"

The Cat and the Parrot

No, surely not. The Cat devoured the Washerman.

The Cat next met the wedding procession of a King: a column of soldiers, and a row of fine elephants two and two. The King said, "O Cat, get away, or my elephants will trample you to death."

Thought the Cat, "I ate a basketful of cakes, I ate my friend the Parrot, I ate the abusive old Woman, I ate the Washerman and his donkey, and shall I blush to eat a beggarly King?"

No, surely not. The Cat devoured the King, and his procession, and his elephants too.

Then the Cat went on until she met a pair of Landcrabs. "Run away, run away, Pussycat!" said the Landcrabs, "or we will nip you!"

"Ha! ha! ha!" laughed the Cat, shaking her sides (fat enough they were by this time), "I ate a basketful of cakes, I ate my friend the Parrot, I ate an abusive old Woman, I ate the Washerman and his donkey, I ate the King and all his elephants, and shall I run away from a Landcrab? Not so, but I will eat the Landcrab too!" So saying, she pounced upon the Landcrabs. Gobble, gobble, slip, slop: in two swallows the Landcrabs went down the Cat's gullet.

But although the Landcrabs slid down the Cat's gullet easily enough, you must know that they are hard creatures, too hard for a Cat to bite; so they took no harm at all. They found themselves amongst a crowd of creatures. There was the King, sitting with his head on his hands, very unhappy; there was the King's newly-wed bride in a dead faint; there was a company of soldiers, trying to form fours, but rather muddled in mind; there was a herd of elephants, trumpeting loudly; there was a donkey braying and the Washerman beating the donkey with a stick; there was the Parrot, whetting his beak on his own claws; then there was the old Woman abusing them all roundly; and last of all, five hundred cakes neatly piled in a corner. The Landcrabs ran round to see what they could find; and they found that the inside of the Cat was quite soft. They could not see anything at all, except by flashes, when the Cat opened her mouth, but they

The Cat and the Parrot

could feel. So they opened their claws, and nip! nip! nip!

"Miaw!" squealed the Cat.

Then came another nip, and another great Miaw! The Landcrabs went on nipping, until they had nipped a big round hole in the side of the Cat. By this time the Cat was lying down, in great pain; and as the hole was very big, out walked the Landcrabs, and scuttled away. Then out walked the King, carrying his bride; and out walked the elephants, two and two; out walked the soldiers, who had succeeded in forming fours-right, by your left, quick march! out walked the donkey, with the Washerman driving him along; out walked the old Woman, giving the Cat a piece of her mind; and last of all, out walked the Parrot, with a cake in each claw. Then they all went about their business, as if nothing had happened; and the Parrot flew back to whet his beak on the branch of the mango-tree.

Notes

Notes

1.—The Talking Thrush

Told by Káshi Prasád, village school, Bhingá, district Bahráich, Oudh.

Man sows cotton-seeds in garden—Phudki bird sees him—Makes her nest of the cotton—Goes to a Behana, and says, "If I bring you cotton, will you card it, and give me half, keeping half yourself?"—He does so—"Now make it into balls" (Piuni)—Does so on the same terms—A Kori spins thread on the same terms—And weaves it into cloth—Similarly a tailor makes it into clothes—She flies to court and sits on a peg—Says the King, "Give me your suit"—She does so, and says, "The King covets my suit"—"Come here, and I will return it"—She comes, and he catches her—"I will cut you in pieces"—"The King will cut me in pieces to-day"—He cuts her up and tells his servant to wash them—"To-day the King is washing and cleaning"—Puts her in a pan of oil—"To-day the King is frying me in oil"—Eats her—"I shall go into the King's stomach"—The Bird puts out its head—Two soldiers attempt to cut it off, and mutilate the King so that he dies.

The *motif* is much the same as in No. 2 of the collection. The pieces of the Thrush speak like the fish in the tale of the "Fisherman and the Jinni" (Burton, "Arabian Nights," Library Edition, I. 59).

2.—The Rabbit and the Monkey

Told by Dankhah Rabha, in the Bhutan Hills. Taken without essential change from *North Indian Notes and Queries*, iv. § 465.

3.—The Sparrow's Revenge

Told by Shin Sahái, teacher of the village school of Dayarhi Chakeri, Etah District. Another version of the *Podná* and the *Podní*, *N.I.N.Q.* iii. 83. Compare the *Valiant Blackbird*, No. 28 below.

Hen Sparrow tells her husband to go into the jungle and fetch firewood to cook *khir* (rice milk)—A *Chamár* kills him—Hen makes carriage of straw, yokes two rats to it, and drives off to take vengeance—Meets a Wolf—"Where are you going?"—"To take vengeance on the Chamár who killed my husband"—"May I help?"—"It will be kind"—Meets a Snake, who salutes her with, "Rám! Rám! Whither away?"—Replies as before, and same thing happens—So with a Scorpion—They arrive at the house of the Chamár—Wolf hides near the river—Snake under pile of cow-dung fuel—Scorpion under the lamp—The Sparrow flies up to the eaves and twitters—Out comes Chamár—Says she, "A friend awaits you near the river." To the river he goes—Wolf seizes him—His wife goes to the heap for fuel—Snake bites her—She calls to her son, "Bring the lamp"—Scorpion stings him—They all die—Hen Sparrow gets another mate, and lives happily ever after.

It is part of the Faithful Animal cycle (Temple, "Wide-awake Stories," 412; Clouston, "Popular Tales and Fictions," i. 223 *seqq.*). This form of tale, in which the weaker animal gets the better of its more powerful oppressor, is common in Indian folk-lore. Compare No. 1 of this collection.

4.—The Judgment of the Jackal

Told by SHIUDAN CHAMAR, of Chaukiya, Mirzápur.
N.I.N.Q. iii. 101.

Merchant puts up at house of Oilman—Oilman ties the horse to his mill—Next morning Merchant asks for it—He replies, "It has run away!"—"But what is that horse?"—"My mill gave birth to it in the night"—Appeal to Siyar Panre, the Jackal—"Go back and I will come"—He bathes in a tank—Delay—They seek him, and find him sitting by the tank—"Why did you delay?"—"Too busy; the tank caught fire, and I have just put it out"—"You are mad; who ever heard of a tank on fire?"—"Who ever heard of a mill bearing a foal?"—Oilman returns horse.

A parallel may be found in the Buddhist *Jātaka*, No. 219 (Cambridge translation, ii. 129), another Version from the Frontier in Swynnerton's "Indian Nights' Entertainment," p. 142. Compare Stumme, *Tunisische Märchen*, vol. ii., Story of an Oilman.

5.—How the Mouse got into his Hole

Told by BISRAM BANYA and recorded by MAHARAJ SINH, teacher of the school at Akbarpur, Faizabad district.

6.—King Solomon and the Owl

Told by MUNSHÍ CHHOTÉ KHÁN, teacher of the village school at Ant, District Sitápur, Oudh.

[A new legend of the Fall.]

Solomon hunts alone—An Owl asks him to receive him—Solomon asks, "Why do you hoot all night?"—"To wake men and women early for prayer: travelling is difficult, for treasure is dearer than life"—"Why do you shake your head?"—"To remind mankind that the world is but a fleeting show, and to show my disapproval of their delight in worldly things"—"Why do you eat no grain?"—"*Adam ate wheat in heaven, and was turned out of it on that account.* Adam prayed, and God sent him into the world, and blessed him to be the father of mankind. If I eat one grain I expect to be cast into hell"—"Why do you drink no water in the world at night?"—"Because Noah's race was drowned in this world in water. If I drink, it would be hard for me to live"—Solomon is pleased, and asks the Owl to remain with him, and advise him on all points.

There is no verse in the original.

All through the eastern world the owl, from its association with graveyards and old ruins, is regarded as a mystic bird, invested with powers of prophecy and wisdom (Crooke, "Popular Religion and Folk-lore of Northern India," i. 279).

7.—The Camel's Neck

Told by BACHÁÚ, a Kasera, or brassfounder, of Mirzápur, North-West Provinces.

Camel practises austerities—Bhagwán is pleased, and appears to him—"Who are you?"—"Lord of the Three Regions"—"Show me your proper form"—Bhagwán appears in his four-handed form (Chaturbhuji)—Camel does reverence—"Ask a boon"—"Let my neck be a *yojan* long"—"Be it so"—The neck becomes eight miles long—He can now graze within a radius of four miles (*sic*)—It rains—He puts his neck in a cave—A pair of Jackals eat his flesh—The Camel dies—A wise man says—

"Álas dókh mahán dekhyo phal kaisá bhayá;
Yátén únt aján, maran lagyo nij karm se."

"Idleness is a great fault: see what was the result of idleness. By this the foolish Camel died, simply owing to his own deeds."

This is one of the very common cycle of tales where the fool comes to ruin in consequence of a stupid wish. In the "Book of Sindibad," it appears as the "Peri and the Religious Man" (Clouston, "Book of Sindibad," 71); La Fontaine has adopted it as the "Three Wishes," and Prior as "The Ladle." The Italian version will be found in Crane, "Italian Popular Tales," 221. The four-hand god is Vishnu in his form as Chaturbhuja.

8.—The Quail and the Fowler

Told by RAMESWAR-PURI, a wandering religious beggar of Kharwá, District Mirzápur.

Fowler catches a Quail—"I'll teach you three things, and if you free me I'll teach you a fourth: (1) Never set free what you have caught; (2) What seems to you untrue you need not believe; (3) What is past you should not trouble about"— He sets the Quail free—Says the Quail, "I have in my stomach a gem weighing 1¼ seers, and worth lakhs of rupees; had you not let me go you would have that gem"—Fowler falls on the ground in misery—Says the Quail, "You forget my teaching: (1) You set me free; (2) You did not ask how a body so light could contain such a gem; (3) You are troubled about what is past"—Flies away—Fowler returns home a wiser man.

Compare the "Laughable Stories of Bar-Hebraeus," E. A. W. Budge (Luzac, 1897), No. 382, where a Sparrow acts as this Quail does. See also the "Three Counsels worth Money" in No. 485.

9.—The King of the Kites

Told by RÁM DÉO, Brahman, of Mirzápur.

Frog and Mouse dispute, each saying he is King of the Kites —The dispute lasts for several years—They refer it to a *Panch* (Committee of Five)—The other three are Bat, Squirrel, Parrot—

They cannot decide—A small Kite appears—Carries off both Frog and Mouse, and eats them—The rest depart—The dispute does not arise again.

The belief that each species of bird and beast has a king of its own is common. Thus, we have a king of the serpents, of mice, of flies, locusts, ants, foxes, cats, and so on (Frazer, "Pausanias," iii. 559). Also see No. 27 of this collection.

10.—The Jackal and the Camel

Told by HAR PRASÁD, Brahman, of Saráya Aghat, District Etah, N.W.P.

Camel grazing, entangles nose-string in a tree—Confused in mind, appeals to Jackal—"Brother, I will free you for one *seer* of flesh"—He agrees—Jackal asks the tongue—"Have you a witness?"—Jackal tries all the beasts, offering half of all he gets—Wolf refuses—Jackal explains that the Camel will die, and they will get all his body—He then agrees, and swears it—Camel opens his mouth, curls back tongue—Jackal cannot catch the tongue—Wolf tries—When the head is well in, Camel closes his jaws—"O *Dâdâ* (father), what is this?"—Says Jackal, "The result of lying," and runs away—Wolf dies.

In Oriental folk-lore the jackal takes the place which the fox occupies in the Western world, and numerous tales are told of his cunning. This fact has formed the base of an argument to prove that the European Beast tales originated from the East (Tawney, "Katha Sarit Ságara," ii. 28).

11.—The Wise Old Shepherd

Told by MUNSHI FAZL KARÍM of Mirzápur.

A Nága (Snake) goes out of his hole to take an airing—Enters the Raja's court—All flee in terror—Raja orders the Snake to be

Notes

killed—The Prince kills it—Snake's wife goes in search—Enters the court and learns his fate—Vows to make his wife also a widow—Coils round the Prince's neck in the night—He dares not stir—Queen-mother goes to see what is the matter—Sees the Snake—Raja sends archers—They prepare to shoot—Snake pleads fair reprisals, and asks that the matter be decided by Panch—They find five Shepherds holding a Panchayat—They all go thither—The men all agree that the Snake is right except one—He asks how many sons has the Snake—"Seven"—"Then you must wait till the Princess has three more, and then you may kill him."

There is a universal taboo in India against killing a snake. When a cobra is slain it is supposed that its mate always avenges its death (Crooke, "Popular Religion and Folk-lore of Northern India," i. 226).

12.—Beware of Bad Company

Told by JAGAT KISHOR, master at the Government School, Gondá, Oudh.

A Swan made friends with a Crow—They fly away from Mánsarowar to find some sport—Perch on a pipal tree under which a pious Raja is worshipping his Thákurji (idol of Rám or Krishna)—Crow drops filth on his head and flies away—He sees the Swan and shoots it—Swan says:—

> "Kák náhin, ham hans hain,
> Mán karat ham bás;
> Dhrisht kág ké mél són,
> Bhayo hamaró nás."

("I am no Crow but a Swan, dwelling in Mán Saròwar; being friend of an ignoble Crow I am destroyed.")

The Crow, as in several tales in this collection, is in Oriental folk-lore the representative of all that is thievish and mischievous.

13.—The Foolish Wolf

Told by MAHÁDEVA PRASÁD, pupil of branch school, Nau Shaharah, District Gonda, Oudh.

Wolf and Ass were friends—Played as described in text—Boy sees Wolf running away from Ass, and says, "What a timid Wolf"—Says the Wolf, "You shall rue it, I'll carry you off to-day"—Boy tells his mother—"Never mind, he won't hurt you"—Hides stone in loin-cloth—Wolf comes for him—Leaves him in his den for the morrow—Goes to play with the Ass—Boy climbs a tree—Wolf finds no Boy—Stands gaping with perplexity—Boy throws stone into his mouth and kills him.

14.—Reflected Glory

Told by MÁTÁ DÍN, assistant teacher, Pili-Bhít district, N.W.P.

A Shepherd had a lame Goat which he beat—It ran away—Fearing the wild beasts, it sat down beside a cave where were footsteps of a Lion—A Jackal comes up—"Rám, Rám, grandfather! I have found food after many days." "Rám, Rám, grandson, I was told to sit here by the owner of these footprints."—"A Lion! if I eat you, he will eat my cubs"—He goes—A Wolf comes, and the same thing happens—The Lion comes—Says the Goat, "By the influence of your footprints I have been safe; beasts came to devour me, and I became your man: they fled." "If you have called yourself my man I will not eat you"—Lion finds an Elephant: "I have a lame Goat; let him go on your back and eat the young leaves as you graze"—He agrees, and the Goat says, "Khoj pakar liyo baran ko hasti mili hai ái gaj mastak achchhi charhi ajayá kopal kháya" ("By betaking myself to the footprints of the great, I have got an Elephant")—Mounting on the Elephant's head, the Goat feeds well on new leaves.

15.—The Cat and the Sparrows

Told by TULSI RÁM, Brahman, of Sadabad, Mathura district. For the *motif*, compare *Jātaka*, No. 333 (translation, vol. iii. p. 71).

16.—The Foolish Fish

Told by HARI CHAND or HEM CHANDI, teacher of a village school, Mirzápur district. A variant of the same, told by SHEO-DÁN, Chamár, Chankiyá, Mirzápur district.

Banya sees Tiger sunk in the mud—Tiger tries him to release him—Swears he will not hurt him or his family—Banya saves him—Says Tiger, "Shall I eat you or your ox?"—Banya protests —Tiger: "It is the way of my family"—Banya says, "Let the Jackal arbitrate"—Jackal asks to see the place the Tiger was in— Then to be shown exactly how he was—The Tiger goes in again, and the Jackal advises the man to go home and leave him.

17.—The Clever Goat

Recorded by MÁTÁ DÍN, assistant teacher, Pili-Bhít district.

18.—A Crow is a Crow for Ever

Told and recorded by SÁHIB RÁM, Brahman, of Nardauli, Etah district.

The verse is:—

> Kág parháe pinjra : parhi gaye cháron Ved :
> Jab sudhi ai kutum ki rahe dhed ke dhed.

"I kept my crow in a cage, and taught him all four Vedas;
When he thought of his family, he became filthy as ever."

19.—The Grateful Goat

Told by BIKKÚ MISRA, Brahman, Achhnérá village, Agra district.

Butcher buys a Goat—"Spare my life, and I will repay you"—He spares him—The Goat goes into the forest and meets a Jackal—"I am going to eat you." "Wait till I get fat in the forest." "Good : look out for me when you come back"—Meets a Wolf—Same thing happens—Finds a temple of Mahádeva—In it are gold coins—Swallows them—Goes to a flower-seller—"Cover me with flowers"—He does so, and the Goat voids two mohurs—Sets out to return—Meets the Wolf—"Have you seen a Goat?" "No"—Meets the Jackal—"Have you seen a Goat?" "Yes, some distance back"—Proceeds to the Butcher, and voids the rest of the coins—The Butcher is grateful, and never kills him as long as he lives.

Agra district. Tales of animals spitting gold are common, as in Grimm's "Three Little Men in the Wood" ("Household Tales," i. 56) and in Oriental Folk-lore (Tawney, "Katha Sarit Ságara," ii. 8, 453, 637; Knowles, "Folk-tales of Kashmir," p. 443).

20. The Cunning Jackal

Told by BAL BÍR PRASÁD, teacher of the school at
Sultánpur, Oudh.

A Jackal sees melons on the other side of a river—Sees a Tortoise—"How are you and your family?" "I am well, but I have no wife." "Why did you not tell me? some people on the other side have asked me to find a match for their daughter." "If you mean it I will take you across"—Takes him across on his back—When the melons are over the Jackal dresses up a jhau-tree as a bride—"There is your bride, but she is too modest to speak till I am gone"—Tortoise carries him back—Calls to the stump—No answer—Goes up and touches it—Finds it is a tree—Vows revenge—As Jackal drinks, catches his leg—"You fool, you have got hold of a stump by mistake; see, here is my leg," pointing to a stump—Tortoise leaves hold—Jackal escapes—Tortoise goes to Jackal's den—Jackal returns and sees the footprints leading into the den—Piles dry leaves at the mouth, and fires them—Tortoise expires.

This is an unpublished variant of the "Jackal and the Crocodile" (Temple, "Wide-awake Stories," 243).

21.—The Farmer's Ass

Told by RÁM SINH, Haidar-Garh, district Barau Banki.

A Washerman has an Ass that brays on hearing a conch-shell, thinks he must have been a saint in a former life, but something went wrong (kahin chuk gaya) and he became an Ass—Names him Tulsi Das—Ass dies—"He was valuable to me," shaves head, performs obsequies, gives feast to clansmen—Goes to shop of a Banya—"Why are you in mourning?" "Tulsi Das, who was a great saint, is dead"—Banya shaves, too—Raja's sepoy asks him why—"Tulsi Das is dead"—Shaves, too—Comrades ask why—Same thing—Same with the chief of the sepoys—The minister, the raja, all shave—Queen asks why—Raja tells her—"But who is Tulsi Das?" "A friend of the minister's"—So the report is traced back to the Washerman, who says, "He was my Ass."

N.I.N.Q., iii. § 104, gives the same tale about an ass named Sobhan (beautiful): told by Shyam Sundar, village accountant of Dudhi, Mirzápur district, recorded by Ahmad Ullah. Compare Temple's "Wide-awake Stories," 'The Death and Burial of poor Hen Sparrow;' Lady Burton's "Arabian Nights," iii. 228, 'The Unwise Schoolmaster who fell in Love by Report;' Jacob's "English Fairy Tales," 'Tetty Mouse and Tatty Mouse,' and *note*, p. 234.

22.—The Parrot Judge

Told by Makund Lál, *Mirzápur.*

A Bird-catcher had a Parrot which knew only two words, Beshak (undoubtedly) and Cheshak (what doubt)—Took it to market, and gave out that it knew Persian, price 5 lakhs of rupees—Nobleman asks it, "Do you know Persian?"—"Cheshak"—Buys it—Puts it in a gold cage, and gives it good food—King one day began to talk to the Parrot in Persian—It could say nothing but these two words—The owner threw it on the ground and killed it.

23.—The Frog and the Snake

Told by Akbar Sháh, *Mánjhi, one of the jungle-folk of Manbasa, Dudhi, Mirzápur, and recorded by Pandit Ramgharíb Chaubé.* N.I.N.Q., iii. § 101.

No change. The King of the Snakes is Vásuki Nága.

24.—Little Miss Mouse

Told by Akbar Sháh, *Mánjhi, of Manbasa, Dudhi, Mirzápur.* N.I.N.Q., iv. § 19.

No change in first part. The music-shop is in the original the house of the Chamár (a caste of labourers and leather-workers), who gives a drum, which is broken by a woman husking rice, who strikes it with a pestle. The crop in the last scene is rice.

25.—The Jackal that Lost his Tail

Told by Parmanand Tiwári, student, Anglo-Sanskrit School, Mirzápur. *N.I.N.Q.*, iv. § 17.

A Kurmi (one of the agricultural tribes) used to go to his field—At noon his wife brought the dinner—Meets Jackal, and all falls out as in tale till the tail is cut off—Jackal returns and finds wife gathering cow-dung—"Your son (*sic*) has cut off my tail, and I must bite you." "He is dead, come to the funeral feast?"—He and his friends come—"To prevent you squabbling, let me tie you up"—Ties them to the cattle pegs, tailless Jackal with specially strong chain—Kurmi comes out with bludgeon—They break their ropes and flee, all but tailless Jackal, which Kurmi kills.

This is connected with the Æsopian fable of "The Fox who Lost his Tail."

26.—The Wily Tortoise

Told by Brij Mohan Lál, second master, High School, Manipuri, N.W.P. The bird is a *Hansa*. *N.I.N.Q.*, iii. § 295.

27.—The King of the Mice

Told and recorded by Babu Gandharab Sinh, of Etah.

Kingdom of Mice—Mouse King and Fox Wazir—All animals of forest did homage—Caravan passed—Camel left behind—Eats the Mouse King's garden—Fox brings him in—Mocks the King—Nose-string gets entangled—King says he is served right—He begs release and promises service—Mouse gnaws string—Camel serves him—Woodcutters find Camel and take him—King sends to fetch them—Demands his Camel—The Woodcutters tell their King—He refuses—King of Mice collects armies and burrows under Woodcutter's treasury — Brings all the money out in charge of a detachment of Mice—Wise man sees it—Covets the money—Old Mouse says, "Why do you covet? our King will give you service"—Goes to the King—The King bids him fetch more of his brethren—With these the Mouse King invades the realm of Woodcutters—Mice undermine the walls of the enemy's fort—Woodcutters' army flee—King of Mice gets back his Camel, and makes the Woodcutter King his vassal.

(The episode of the wise man seems to be interpolated, as the men play no part in the attack.)

Another version in *N.I.N.Q.*, iii. § 292, told by THÁKUR UMRÁO SINH of Sonhár, Etah district, N.W.P. For Kings of Animals, compare No. 9 of this book.

28.—The Valiant Blackbird

Told by WAZÍRAN, a Mohammedan servant of Mirzápur, and recorded by MIRZA MUHAMMAD BEG.

A Podna (weaver bird) and his mate lived in a tree—The Raja catches the wife—Podna builds carts of reeds, yokes pairs of frogs, makes kettle-drum, armed with piece of reed, sets out drumming —Meets a Cat—"Where are you going?" "Sarkande ki to gári, do mendak jote jaen, Raja mári Podni, ham bair bisahne jaen" ("My carriage is of reed with two frogs yoked thereto; the King has seized my Podni; I go to take my revenge"). "May I go with you?" "Get into my car"—Meets in same way Ants, Rope and Club, River—Drives into King's courtyard and demands Podni—King orders him to be shut in henhouse—"Nikal billi, teri bári. Kán chhor, kanpati mári" ("Come out, Cat, your turn now: come out of my ear and hit them on the head")—Cat comes out and kills fowls—Next night shut in stable—"Niklo rassi, aur sonte tumhari bari. Kan chhor, kanpati mari"—Rope ties horses and Club kills them—Next night shut in with elephants—"Niklo chiunti tumhári bári. Kán chhor, kanpati mári"—Ants run up trunks and sting their brains—Next night tied to the Raja's bed

—"Niklo darya teri bári. Kán chhor, kanpati mári"—River begins to drown King and bed—"For God's sake, take your wife and go."

Here, as in other tales of this collection, we have the incident of the Helping Animals, for which see Tawney, "Katha Sarit Ságara," ii. 103, 596; Crooke, "Popular Religion and Folk-lore of Northern India," ii. 202. See *N.I.N.Q.*, iii. § 173.

29.—The Goat and the Hog

Told by Súraj Singh, assistant master of the Kándhla school, district Muzafarnagar, N.W.P. See *N.I.N.Q.*, iv. § 430.

Goat and Hog friends—Goat goes to seek his fortune—Enters shop of a Banya—Eats all he can find—Goes into inner room—Banya returns—Little girl cries for sugar—Goes in to get some—Goat says, "Ek sing anrur ganrur; dusri sing meri, soni marhawal. Banya beti awo nahin, dhenruki phoron" ("One of my horns is twisted, one is gilt with gold. Don't come in, Banya girl, or I will tear your stomach open")—Runs out—Father sends for the Kotwal—Same thing—Prays to him—Goat comes out: "I want sweetmeats, ornaments for my head, neck, feet, horns, tail"—Gives them, putting on all the jewels he has in pawn—Goat shows all this to the Hog—Hog goes to try his luck—Knew no verses—No one frightened—Banya drives him out with stick and dogs.

30.—The Parrot and the Parson

Told by Bachau Kasera, Mirzápur. *N.I.N.Q.*, v. § 72.

Banker taught his parrot to speak—A Sadhu passed by—Quoth Parrot, "Salaam, Maharáj, how can I get out?" "Let me ask my Guru"—Guru when asked swooned—Sádhu told Parrot what had happened, and apologised for not being able to help—"I understand," says Parrot—Feigns death—Cage opened.

31.—The Lion and the Hare

Told by Suryabali, Mirzápur.

No change. The verse is:—

> Biná budhí ke bágh biláná :
> Kharhá san kahún bágh maráná.

32.—The Monkey's Bargains

Told and recorded by Rameswar-Puri, teacher, Khairwá village school, district Mirzápur.

The Story of Gangá Bûrhi (name of the old woman). No change in the incidents, except that the cowherd is grinding corn, and the last sentence is added. The verses are:—

> Wáh, jangle men se lakari láyá,
> Wáh, lakari main burhyá ko dinh,
> Burhiyá monkon roti dinh,
> Wáh rotiyá main tokôn dinh
> 5 Kyá tun mokôn mataki na degá?

"Hullo! I brought fuel from the forest. (2) I gave it to the old woman. (3) The old woman gave me cake. (4) I gave that cake to thee. (5) Wilt not thou give me jugs?"

> 4 U roti main kohrá ko dinh,
> Kohrá monkôn metuki dinh,
> U metuki main tokôn dinh,
> Kyá tu mujhko makkhan na degá?

"I gave that cake to the Potter. (5) The Potter gave me an earthen vessel. (6) I gave that earthen vessel to thee. (7) Wilt not thou give me butter?"

> 4 Wáh roti main kumhará ko dinh,
> Kumhará monkon metuki dinh,
> Wáh metuki main gwálin ko dinh
> Gwálin monkon londi dinh,
> Wáh londi main tokôn dinh,
> Kyá tu monkôn ek bail bhí na degá?

Notes

"(6) I gave that earthen vessel to the cowherd's wife. (7) The cowherd's wife gave me a lump of butter. (8) I gave that lump to thee. (9) Wilt not thou give me an Ox?"

The others are not given, except the last lines:—

> Baj meri dholaki dhámak dhûn;
> Râni ke badle ái tun.

"O my drum, make sounds like *dhámak dhûn*: thou art come in exchange for a Queen."

33.—The Monkey's Rebuke

Told and recorded by LÁLÁ BHAWÁNÍ DÍN, teacher of Majhgáon district Hamirpur.

A Banya sold milk mixed with water—Earns 100 rupees—Sets out for home—Stops to wash at a tank—Lays the bag down—Monkey takes the bag up a tree—Drops 50 rupees in the tank—Throws down the bag to the man—"You sold half water and half milk: therefore I have thrown half your money into this tank"—Banya goes home a better man.

34.—The Bull and the Bullfinch

Told by PANDIT JAGANNÁTH PRASÁD, master of Marári Kalán village school, and recorded by Pandit Madhuban, second master of the same, Unáo district, Oudh.

Khusat Bird and Bull—The rest as in the story, save that "the Almighty King of the Universe" promises his help to the Lion—Bull tells Bird—Bird says, "Did not I warn you? still I will help"—Tells him that he has dreamt a marriage has been arranged for himself with Mahadeva's spouse—They apply to Mahadeva for explanation—Mahadeva thinks, "If I say visions are real things, this Bird will claim my wife"—So says, "Dreams go by contraries: go home and don't be foolish."

See the value of friendship.

35.—The Swan and the Crow

Told by LÁLA SHANKAR LÁL, village accountant, and recorded by CHANGAN SINH, master of the school at Chamkari, Etah district, N.W.P.

No change, except Wazir for Judge and Gayá for Jerusalem. The Judge is a Hindu, and the Crow promises to take his father's bones to the sacred city of Gayá, in Bengal.

36.—Pride shall have a Fall

Told by AKBAR SHÁH, Mánjhi, one of the jungle-folk of Manbasa, district Mirzápur.

No change. The animal with one eye is supposed to be cunning and uncanny (Crooke, "Popular Religion and Folk-lore of Northern India," ii. 37, 51). Compare No. 37 of this collection.

37.—The Kid and the Tiger

Told by AKBAR SHÁH, Mánjhi, and recorded by PANDIT RAM-GHARÍB CHAUBÉ. A favourite nursery tale of the Kharwárs of Mirzápur.

Tigress and She-goat great friends—Tigress has two cubs, Goat four kids named Khurbhur, Muddil, Goddil, and Nathil—Tigress thinks: "It is hard that I have only two, and the Goat has four: suppose I eat two of hers to make things even"—Asks the Goat to let one kid sleep with her—Only Khurbhur consents—Khurbhur puts one of her cubs in his place—She eats it—Puts a stone in his place—She breaks her teeth—One-eyed Tiger calls—Tells a "story": "When I eat goats, all the four kids are one mouthful" —Khurbhur says, "When you come to eat us, Muddil will hold

Notes

your head, Nathil the fore-paws, Goddil the hind-paws, Khurbhur will cut off your head, if mother holds the light"—Tiger runs away—Meets six more—They go to Goat's house—Khurbhur climbs tree—They jump and miss him—They climb one on another, One-eye at bottom—Khurbhur says, "Mother, a lump of mud to throw in his eye"—One-eye jumps—They fall—They run away, and trouble the goats no more.

The one-eyed animal appears in No. 35 of this collection.

38.—The Stag, the Crow, and the Jackal

Told and recorded by Balbír Prasád, *Brahman, of Mirzápur.*

Stag and Crow are friends—Jackal covets Stag—Says, "A crow is not a friend for you; choose a denizen of earth like me"—They become friends—Jackal leads him to snare—Stag is trapped—"I cannot help you, because there is leather in the snare, and it is the Ekádashi (eleventh day of the lunar fortnight) when I fast"—Crow advises him to feign death—He does so, and escapes.

39.—The Monkey and the Crows

Told by Sariju Prasád, *teacher of the school at Subhikha, Bahraich district, Oudh.*

Crows build nests in a cotton-tree (*semal*)—In the rains a Monkey arrives soaking—Said the Crows, "We build nests with only a beak: can you not make a better with two hands and two feet?" "Wait till morning"—Then he tears down their nests—"Good advice given to a fool only kindles his malice."

40.—The Swan and the Paddy-bird

Told by Devi Dín, student, and recorded by Badari Prasád, of the school at Musanagar, Cawnpur district.

No change. The lake in the original is the famous Mana Sarovar lake in Tibet. The Swan at the end repeats this couplet:—

> Bit chhoto, chit saugun, bit men chit na samác :
> So murak binsat sadan, jirni bakuli nariyar kháe.

("Desire is one thing, capacity is another. The desire exceeds the power. Thus die the foolish, as did the Paddy-bird when she tried to eat the cocoa-nut.")

The Paddy-bird is the Bagla, or Bagula, a sort of small heron (*Ardea torra*), which frequents the banks of ponds and catches little fish and frogs. In folk-lore, from its quaint appearance, it is the type of demure cunning, and a sanctimonious rogue ascetic is often compared to it.

Compare a similar tale of a crane: *Jātaka*, No. 236 (Cambridge translation, ii. 161).

41.—What is a Man?

Told by Shibbá Sinh Gaur, Brahman, resident in Saharanpur, N.W.P.

No change, except that the order of the animals is Elephant, Camel, Ox.

Another version makes the man a carpenter—He goes away and makes a cage—Induces the Lion to enter—Leaves him to starve.

The complaints of the animals against men form the subject of a very amusing Hindustani book derived from the Persian, the Akhwán-us-safa.

Notes

42.—The Wound and the Scar

Told by SHAIKH FARÍD AHMAD, and recorded by the teacher of the village school, Barhauli, district Bahraich, Oudh.

No change, except the Wound is dealt by the Woodman's axe, at the command of the Lion, when first he visits him after the sickness. The verses are—

> Samman dhaga prem ka jin toryo chatkay
> Jore se na jurat hai, aut ganth par jay.

43.—The Cat and the Parrot

Told by BISESHAR DAYÁL, Banya (or corn-chandler), of Bindki, district Fatehpur, N.W.P., and recorded by PANDIT BALDEO PRASÁD, teacher of the Tahsili school, Bindki.

No change, except the Parrot says, "I am sitting on the branch of a mango-tree and getting a bill made." Number of cakes not given. And after meeting the Raja, the Cat meets (1) four young of the wild cow (Surahgáya), which she eats, and (2) a pair of Surahgáya, which fall upon her, and tear her stomach open, when all those she has eaten troop out.

Here, as in other tales of this collection, the Parson is the Guru or spiritual adviser of pious Hindus.

Printed in Great Britain
by Amazon